W9-APW-133

TOP PROS

PECT

PAUL VOLPONI

CAROLRHODA BOOKS
MINNEAPOLIS

Carolrhoda Books
A division of Lerner Publishing Group, Inc.
241 First Avenue North
Minneapolis, MN 55401 USA

For reading levels and more information, look up this title at www.lernerbooks.com.

Cover images: © ostill/Shutterstock.com, (football player); © foxie/Shutterstock.com, (brush strokes). Interior images: © Tatiana Kasyanova/Shutterstock.com.

Main body text set in Bembo Std regular 12.5/17.
Typeface provided by Monotype Typography.

Library of Congress Cataloging-in-Publication Data

Names: Volponi, Paul.
Title: Top prospect / Paul Volponi.
Description: Minneapolis : Carolrhoda Books, 2016. | Summary: "Travis, a pre-teen quarterback with big potential, gets the opportunity of a lifetime when the coach of Gainesville University football program offers him a scholarship before Travis even gets to high school" —Provided by publisher.
Identifiers: LCCN 2015035255 | ISBN 9781467794336 (lb : alk. paper) | ISBN 9781512408874 (eb pdf)
Subjects: | CYAC: Football—Fiction. | Ability—Fiction. | Scholarships—Fiction. | Schools—Fiction.
Classification: LCC PZ7.V8877 To 2016 | DDC [Fic]—dc23

LC record available at http://lccn.loc.gov/2015035255

Manufactured in the United States of America
1-38498-20358-3/8/2016

This novel was inspired by
several middle-school athletes
who were offered college football
scholarships prior to entering
high school.

It is dedicated to the loving
memory of my nephew Jesse, who
left us too soon.

-PROLOGUE-

If you ask me what I love most, the answer would be football. Hands down. Not the whole game—the running, blocking, and tackling parts. Those things are all right. I'm talking about playing quarterback. Calling the play in the huddle and then leading a team up to the line of scrimmage. It feels like the entire world is hanging on my voice. And when "Hut, hut" springs from my vocal cords, twenty-two football players start flying in every direction. Sometimes the play's moving in fast-forward, difficult to see. Other times, when I'm in the zone, the game moves in slow motion. That's when everything comes easy and natural.

Don't get me wrong. There's pressure in playing quarterback too. Lots of it. Pressure to read the defense for a dozen disguised blitzes, to find the hot receiver, and to deliver a tight-spiral pass into the smallest of windows. Never mind the pressure to win—whether that comes from inside myself or from other people.

The center snaps me the ball, and I feel for the

leather laces, getting the best grip possible. Then I take my three-step drop, with a protective pocket of offensive linemen forming around me. Sometimes I don't see an open receiver. A clock ticks down inside my head. It's a warning that I can't hold onto the football forever, not without getting sacked. As the defense closes in and the pocket begins to collapse, I feel myself getting smaller, shrinking inside my shoulder pads. But I scramble for a seam or hole to escape through, to keep that precious play alive. Even when a defensive lineman—as big as a house—blocks out the sun in front of me, I wouldn't trade playing my position for anything. Because after I take that hit, as long as I get back on my feet, I'm still the quarterback.

CHAPTER I

My name is Travis Gardner. If you follow football, you've probably heard about me. Two years ago, while I was still in the seventh grade, I met Elvis Goddard, the head coach for the Gainesville Fightin' Gators. He'd come to recruit my older brother, Carter, who was a senior tight end at Beauchamp High School. And in case you didn't know, Coach Goddard, the King of College Football, had won two national championships at Gainesville University.

My family lives in a small city called Alachua—pronounced a-*latch*-u-a, like the latch on your front door lock. It's just a twenty-minute drive from the university's campus, with the shadow of Gator football hanging over everything here.

One April afternoon, Coach Goddard actually stepped across our welcome mat. Just being close to him felt incredible. Before that, I'd only seen Coach G. on TV or from seats in the top tier of the Gators' stadium, whenever Carter and I could save up enough money to buy tickets.

Coach G. stood with his wide shoulders arched back. He was tall and lean, with his right leg a little stiffer than his left after suffering an injury during his pro career in Dallas. On his feet, he wore a pair of silver snakeskin boots that came to a sharp point at the toe. Galaxy, our black lab, launched into a barking fit, getting down low and beginning to growl.

"Sorry, Coach. He gets this way with strangers sometimes," said Carter, grabbing Galaxy by the collar and dragging him away into the bedroom we shared.

"He's protecting his territory. That's all. Or maybe it's these boots. They're diamondback *ratt-lers*," Coach G. said in a southern drawl and then started to grin. "You know, I actually prefer gator skin. But I suppose they'd run me out of my job in Gainesville if I ever covered my feet in that."

Coach G. was in his mid-forties, with a smooth-skinned face that made him look much younger. I didn't think anyone could be more impressed by him than Carter and me, until I noticed Mom breathing faster than normal and smiling at every word out of his mouth.

Coach sank into the red cracked-leather recliner, the one that used to be Dad's favorite chair. My parents had been divorced for almost two years. Dad was living in California with his new wife and *her* teenage son. Mom didn't date much. After cleaning people's teeth all day as a dental hygienist, she came home to what she called "the most important unpaid job of my life." That was taking care of Carter and me.

Carter and Mom sat on the sofa opposite Coach, with a small glass table in between them. There was enough room on the sofa's cushions to sit three across. But I parked myself on the sofa arm closest to Coach G.

"Now, Carter, I know we've been late in recruiting you. I understand you've had a few scholarship offers already, some from other schools in Florida. But my staff and I were recently watching video of another player on your team. And every time he broke off a big run, it was you throwing the key block. I told my assistants, 'Forget about the ball carrier. Who's that tight end clearing the way?' And, well, here I am," Coach said before taking a bite from one of Mom's homemade walnut brownies.

My eyes stayed glued to the two huge National Championship rings Coach wore. The one on his right hand was gold, with blue sapphires forming a football in its center. The number *1*, set in diamonds, sparkled in the middle of those sapphires. The ring on his left hand was silver, decorated with the head of an emerald green gator grinning with a mouth full of jeweled teeth.

"That's probably the thing I do best, clearing the way for whoever's coming behind me," Carter said. "I've been practically living in the weight room, getting stronger. And I've been practicing my pass routes too, working on my hands to become a better receiver."

"I sense that hunger in you. It's exactly what I'm looking for in a recruit. You're not satisfied with your game, and striving to achieve more," Coach said. A loud clap of his hands sent Galaxy into another barking fit from the bedroom. "So, *Mom*, wouldn't you like to have peace of mind, knowing your son is attending a top university just a short car ride away? A four-year scholarship with living accommodations, books, and food is worth almost two hundred thousand dollars. That can be quite a burden on the budget of a single-parent household. But that's what a commitment to Gator football can get Carter."

"And you'll look after Carter while he's there?" Mom asked, resting her coffee cup on a chipped saucer. "He's never really been away from home before, not even to sleepaway camp. He's still a boy in lots of ways."

"Not true, Mom," Carter protested, blushing.

"I watch over *all* of my players as if they were my own flesh and blood. So don't give that a second thought," said Coach, slapping Carter on the knee and giving him a wink, as if to let him know that's how all mothers acted.

After a short pause, Coach lifted up his hands, letting a stream of sunlight pouring through the window shine across his rings. "Carter, how'd you like to come to Gainesville? Help me and your future teammates earn a third one of these?"

Then Coach took the ring from his left hand and put it onto Carter's finger.

I jumped up off the arm of the sofa, wanting to scream, "Yes! Yes!"

Only, Coach wasn't asking *me*.

"I'd like it more than anything, to be a Gator," my brother answered. "I've wanted it for a long time."

Carter and Mom nodded to each other, and then my brother hugged her tight.

"I'm so proud of you, Carter," she said, with her eyes starting to tear up.

Coach rose from the recliner and stuck his hand out to Carter, who, at six-foot-five, stood a couple of inches taller.

At five-eleven, I was already the tallest boy in my class. I had a bet with Carter too: one day, I'd be even bigger than him. We were super-competitive that way, battling over things like whose hair would turn blonder during the summer.

"Congratulations, son. Glad to have you aboard," said Coach G., as the two of them shook on it. "You can file your official paperwork tomorrow."

While he was still wearing Coach's ring, Carter and me exchanged high fives, low fives, and fives at every level in between. And I didn't pull a single turkey on him—planting the bottom of my fist on his open palm with my thumb sticking out.

"You should see Carter's hands, Coach. They're like flypaper now. The ball just sticks in them. I've been throwing to him every day in our backyard," I said. "I'm quarterback on my Pop Warner team. I've played that position ever since Pee Wee football, and made the all-star team every season."

"A quarterback, huh? All right, go grab a ball. Let's see," said Coach G.

For me, that was like Christmas coming in April. So I raced into our bedroom for a football.

There wasn't much space out back. We had maybe twenty yards of length and fifteen yards of width for Carter to run patterns, mostly buttonhooks and quick outs.

I was pretty nervous to throw in front of Coach G. He'd sent a pair of my favorite quarterbacks to the NFL. One of them had even won the Heisman Trophy as the country's top college player. My first two passes sailed over Carter's head, with Galaxy spinning in circles from behind our bedroom window, trying to bird-dog each one.

"Just lower your release point, Travis," Coach said, mimicking my throwing motion. "You're letting go of the ball too high in your arc. You probably have too much adrenaline pumping. Calmness and execution— those are the things I preach to my quarterbacks. It's how I played the position."

Calmness and execution, I repeated to myself. So I gripped the ball a little looser, took a deep breath, and focused on my release. After that, I must have hit Carter with thirty straight passes, right on his jersey number.

"Nice hands, Carter. I recruited the right player today," said Coach G. "And, Travis, you've got a lot of zip in that left arm. Keep at it and you might be a Gator one day yourself. Send me some video of one of your games. I'll point out some things for you to work on."

Hearing those words put a smile on my face that didn't wipe off for a while.

A few minutes later, Coach Goddard's SUV pulled away from the curb in front of our house, with us all waving good-bye. Then Mom swiveled her hips and said in a deep voice like an announcer's, "Ladies and gentlemen, Coach Elvis has left the building."

Back inside, Carter and me almost fought over who'd sit in the recliner first. I think we both wanted to sink into the same spot where Coach G. had been. That's where Carter was stationed when he called Dad on his cell. Only, my brother had to leave a voice message when Dad didn't pick up.

"Big news! I picked a college. You won't believe which one. Call me."

Hours went by without a reply from Dad. I knew Carter wasn't about to leave a second message. We'd both been there too many times, waiting and waiting on him, like everything else in his world was more important than us. Dad finally called at about ten o'clock that night— seven o'clock California time. Carter was stretched out on his bed with his laptop, looking at all the different subjects you could major in at Gainesville, when he answered.

"I'm going to be a Gator! We've been celebrating big-time here," Carter told Dad, before I stepped into the bathroom to wash up for bed.

Carter gave him all of the highlights, except for the one I wanted to hear. So I took the toothbrush from my mouth and called out to Dad, "Ask Carter who played quarterback for him in the backyard!"

Carter listened to Dad's response and then said, "No, no, Travis threw great. Coach Goddard even said so. Of course, I'd already accepted the scholarship. But I still wanted to show off my receiving."

I normally talked with Dad once a week, usually on the weekend. He hadn't been back to Florida in over a year. He'd been busy with his job as an insurance salesman and, I guess, his new family.

"All right, I love you too," said Carter. "Yeah, I'll tell Travis. 'Bye."

Carter buried his phone inside the pants pocket of his sweats and went back to his laptop.

"So?" I asked. "What are you supposed to tell me?"

"Oh," said Carter, looking up from the computer screen. "Dad says it's hard for a lefty to make it at quarterback. He thinks you should find another position."

"*What?*" I said, slamming a handful of dirty clothes down into my hamper. "No coach ever said that to me."

Carter just shrugged his shoulders and clicked his mouse pad. Coach G. didn't care that I was left-handed. And Dad didn't know a thing about football compared to *him*.

CARTER'S TAKE

Travis is constantly trying to hitch a ride on where I'm going, on anything I've earned. He's always finding some built-up reason why he contributed to *my* success. It gets really annoying sometimes. But whenever Dad's involved, I try to cut Travis some slack. I took a big hit when Dad left. I guess Travis, being younger, took an even bigger one. I could see that Dad's comment about lefty quarterbacks bothered him. That was my fault. I should have never even told him. So I sucked it up and said, "Hey, Trav—good job. You really did hit me right on the numbers with most of those passes." And I felt better when his face broke out in a half-smile.

CHAPTER 2

The next day, I was tossing a football with some friends in the park. Damon Wilson, who played on my Pop Warner team, had joined me and a few other guys. In my mind, I didn't have a *real* best friend my own age. No big reason why—I just didn't. I'd always try to spend time around Carter and his friends, whenever he'd let me. But if I had to pick somebody like that, Damon would have been the closest to it. He was a big, stocky kid who'd played on my offensive line for a couple of years, protecting me from getting sacked.

I was still riding high over throwing in front of Coach G.

"I swear he worked on my mechanics for something like thirty seconds. That's it. Fixing my release point and stuff," I said, before taking a pretend snap and dropping back. "After that, I was passing like a pro. That's how much better he is than any of the coaches we've ever had."

I raised the ball up to my left ear as my eyes darted

back and forth along a row of apple trees, maybe twenty-five yards away.

"That's probably why his name's *God*-ard," Damon said. "He's like a coaching god."

"It's a *coincidence*," argued another kid. "Coach had that name from when he was born."

"I don't know about any of that," I said, focusing on the narrowest tree. "I only know the results."

Then I released the tightest spiral of my life. I watched the football slice straight through the air like an arrow, hitting the trunk of that oak dead-center. There were *ooohs* and *aaahs* from every kid there. I always had a strong arm. But suddenly, I felt like a different player, better and more confident.

"Hey, go stand by that same tree," I told the kid who'd argued against Coach G. "Let me see if I can knock an apple off your head with this football."

Everybody laughed over that, even the kid I'd said it to. But part of me wasn't joking. I believed I could do it.

A few minutes later, Carter passed by with one of his Beauchamp teammates. All of my friends wanted to get a game of touch going, especially one with Carter, an almost-Gator, in it. Carter and his teammate didn't want to risk getting hurt against a bunch of kids. But they each agreed to play all-time QB for one of the teams, while we did all the running. That got under my skin, because I knew I had better skills.

Carter's teammate didn't have much of an arm, missing on five straight passes for our side.

"Let's try something different. Pitch the ball out to me for a running play," I told the Beauchamp guy in our huddle.

When he turned his head away, I drew an L with my finger on the front of my shirt for Damon to see. That was the diagram for Damon to run a down-and-out pattern.

I took the pitch and ran a few steps before I threw on the brakes.

"Watch out! It's a pass!" Carter screamed to his guys.

Damon made his cut and was running wide open. I lofted him a high, soft one over the tree branches. He caught the football in stride. When Damon crossed the second cement path for a touchdown, he spiked it. For me, that was the last word on who should have been playing quarterback for our team from the beginning.

● ● ●

That week, Mike Harkey, Gainesville's strength and conditioning coach, phoned Carter. He invited my brother down to the football complex on campus to see the Gators' multi-million dollar weight room and training facility. I practically begged Carter to let me tag along. But for two days he said no and wouldn't budge.

"This isn't kiddy play time, Travis. This is serious. My future," he told me.

"Mom, Carter's acting selfish," I said, trying to play her against him.

But she backed up Carter on everything.

"Your brother has to worry about making a good impression, not looking after you," she said.

So I kept quiet on the whole idea for a few days. Then, the Saturday morning when Carter was headed there, I put on a Gainesville football jersey and used my body to block the front door.

"Come on. *Please.* Players my age don't get chances like this. Maybe I can pick up some lifting techniques, move ahead of other kids," I said, praying he'd take pity on me.

Carter exhaled and put his hands on his hips.

"If I say yes, you won't get in the way?" he asked.

"I won't. I promise."

"You won't pick up any weights? Drive Coach Harkey crazy with questions?" Carter continued, as I accepted each condition. "You understand that this is *my* meeting, not *yours?*"

"I get it, completely," I said, opening the door for us.

Mom needed the car to go to her job at the dental office. So we hopped a downtown bus that took us past Beauchamp High, my school—Westside Middle—and then to University Avenue, where we caught a second bus to the campus.

From the outside, the football complex looked like a fancy hotel: tall sheets of glass, palm trees, a smooth marble column, and a bronze statue of a gator. Inside, the lobby was decked out in the Gators' orange and blue, with life-size photos of Gainesville's all-time greatest players lining the walls.

"Someday, my picture's going to be up there," Carter whispered to me.

"Think so?" I said, almost as a challenge.

"Long before yours ever will," he said with confidence.

Then we came to a pair of crystal footballs, each in its own glass case. Those were the trophies for Coach Goddard's two national championships. The light sparkled and shined off them both, casting two rainbows on the wall behind.

"I don't even know how to describe what I'm seeing," I said.

"You don't," replied Carter. "You just appreciate the beauty of it. And work hard to take that same ride one day."

On the other side of the automatic sliding glass doors was a huge weight room, bigger than my middle school's entire gym. It had every workout machine and weight set you could think of. The hundreds of fluorescent lights shining down from the ceiling made it look like some kind of workout heaven.

Carter spotted Harkey kneeling beside a weight bench. When Harkey stood up to greet us, I wasn't that impressed with him physically. He was short with a big barrel chest and stubby arms. He reminded me of the fire hydrant on the street outside our house. I tried hard not to laugh. Because somewhere in the back of my mind, I had the image of Galaxy walking up to Harkey, sniffing at him, and then lifting his leg.

"Good to meet you, Carter," said Harkey, shaking his hand. "Who's this young stud wearing the right jersey?"

"This is my little brother, Travis," he said, as Harkey offered me his hand next.

"His *younger* brother," I countered.

Without showing any effort, Harkey nearly broke my hand inside his steel grip. And I started to rethink my first impression of him.

"So, Carter, how much?" he asked.

Carter seemed confused for a second. "How much weight can I lift?"

"No. How much of a price are you willing to pay?" Harkey asked. "See that sign on the wall?"

It read: *BLOOD, SWEAT, AND TEARS.*

"Go ahead. Touch it, Carter," said Harkey, picking up a blue binder from his desk a few feet away.

Carter ran his hand over the sign. Then I touched it too.

"You know why those letters are raised?" asked Harkey.

We both shook our heads.

"So you can really feel it. So they're not just words," he said. "Everything you want, everything you gain, you pay a price for. Blood, sweat, and tears—that's what lives in here. It comes before all of the glory out on the football field. A scholarship doesn't *entitle* you to anything. Egos don't survive in this room. The players who succeed are afraid to fail, to lose their starting jobs. They outwork everybody else. Now, are you willing to reach deep inside, scrape the bottom of your soul to pay that price?"

"Absolutely," said Carter, without hesitating.

I would have answered exactly the same way.

"Well, we'll see. Here's a workout schedule for you to follow at home and in your gym at school," Harkey said, handing Carter the binder. "We've had players from Beauchamp High before. They weight-train okay over there. You look like you're carrying some decent flesh. But you'll be a different animal when I get through with you."

That's when I puffed out my chest and tightened my abs beneath my jersey. Only, Harkey didn't seem to notice.

* * *

Dad was supposed to spend five days in Florida for Carter's high school graduation. That was *his* idea. We'd planned a day at Disney World, one on Daytona Beach—which is awesome in early June—and one to go deep-sea fishing. It was supposed to make up for Dad not coming to visit us in more than a year—for him driving his stepson to high school swim meets up and down the coast of California on weekends while he missed nearly two entire seasons of our football games.

Then, less than a week before Dad's visit, he called Carter's phone. When he heard me in the background, he asked my brother to put the call on speaker.

"Here's the situation, guys. My company needs me to make some presentations at an insurance conference in Columbus, Ohio," Dad said, in a slow and steady voice that picked up speed the longer he talked. "Unfortunately, the meat of that conference is during the days we had planned together. In fact, the conference actually runs through your graduation ceremony, son. What I can do is fly out of Columbus early in the morning and just go missing for a while. I'll watch you graduate in the afternoon, maybe have a nice celebration lunch at a place close to the airport, and then fly right back out again."

"It's that important?" asked Carter, staring at the phone in his hand.

"Your graduation?" answered Dad. "I should hope so. It is to me. That's why I'm willing to jump through hoops to get there."

"No, I meant the conference," said Carter, shifting his eyes to mine.

I just shook my head and put my hands over my ears. But I could still make out parts of what Dad said after that: "the economy . . . lucky to have this job . . . you'll see when you have bosses." That's when I started humming to myself, muffling out the rest.

* * *

The day Dad flew in, he never came to our house. That was probably because any talk between him and Mom had become an argument waiting to happen. Instead, Dad met us at the ceremony. The auditorium at Beauchamp High isn't big enough to seat five hundred graduates and their families. So the school rented out the main hall on the campus of Gainesville U. Dad stood waiting for us outside the hall, wearing a business suit and a red-striped tie. He looked the same as I remembered, except for a few gray hairs and some extra weight around his midsection.

I'd had the idea of running up to hug Dad. But when I saw him standing there, it just didn't feel right. Besides, his arms weren't opened wide. They were hanging down at his sides.

For the first few minutes, Carter, dressed in his cap and gown, got all of Dad's attention.

"Son, I just can't believe they gave you a scholarship here," he said, draping his right arm around Carter's shoulder. "They obviously know real talent when they see it."

Dad handed me his camera and asked for a photo of him and Carter.

When I finished, Mom took the camera from me and said, "Now you get into this one too, Travis. I know your father wants a picture with both his boys."

"That's right, Travis," Dad said, pulling me in close, inside of his other arm. "One day you'll be grown like your brother. If you work as hard as Carter, it'll be your turn in the spotlight."

Dad still had more than an inch in height on me, while Carter towered over us both. When Mom showed us the photo, it reminded me of Mount Rushmore, with the heads shrinking down from left to right.

After a while, Carter had to get into line with the rest of the graduates. That left me as the only buffer between Mom and Dad. I sat between them in the hall. I was talking mostly to Dad. But I was trying not to ignore Mom, either.

"You know, Travis, you've got a great body to be a swimmer. You've got length and a lot of lean muscle," said Dad, taking his nose out of the graduation program and looking at me over the top of his reading glasses. "I've seen plenty of high school swimmers lately, and you have the build. Ever think of trying out for the swim team when you get to Beauchamp?"

"Nah, I'm going to stick with football," I told him, making a throwing motion with my left arm. "If I'm on the water, it'll be 'cause I'm fishing."

"Don't worry. We'll reschedule that deep-sea trip," he said, almost like an apology. "But if it's definitely going to be football, you might think about becoming a receiver or a tight end like Carter. Quarterback's one of those singular positions. A team can only start one at a time. The odds of making it are much tougher. On top of that, you're a southpaw."

Before I could say anything, the music started and we all stood up as the graduates marched into the hall. There were a bunch of boring speeches from the stage that took almost an hour and a half to get through. The only highlight came when I killed a monster fly that had been dive-bombing us, smashing him flat against the back of the seat in front of me with a rolled-up program. Finally, one by one, the graduates got called up to receive their diplomas. When the principal announced "Carter Gardner" and my brother walked across the stage, I made it a point to clap louder and longer than anyone, especially Dad.

CHAPTER 3

Over the summer before eighth grade, I shot up an inch, to six-foot-even. I put on some muscle too, and got up to a hundred and sixty pounds, pumping iron with Carter three times a week.

I didn't see Coach Goddard again until August, on the morning of Carter's first official college football practice. Mom had the morning free because she was working the late shift at her dental office that day. She liked football more than any mother I knew, so I didn't have to ask twice before she agreed to drive down to Gainesville. We were among the first in line, getting there about an hour before the gates opened. When they did, Mom and me hurried inside and grabbed two field-level seats in the front row. The Gators don't practice in their stadium. That's only for real games. They have a separate practice facility. Even on a Wednesday morning, nearly two thousand fans were there to watch. But that's a Fightin' Gators crowd for you—insanely passionate about its team.

Carter was one of the first players on the field, along with a few of the receivers. My skin tingled as I wished I could be out there too.

"*Woo-hoo!* That's my son! Number eighty-five!" Mom hollered at the top of her lungs.

I could see Carter fighting back a smile as his teammates poked at him. The practice started with a few wind sprints. Surprisingly, the quarterback hadn't taken the field yet. Carter threw a pass to his roommate, Alex Moore, missing him by a mile. Then Alex did the same on the pass back to Carter.

"Honey, they'd be better off with you throwing the ball," Mom joked.

Somehow that was all the encouragement I needed. I jumped the short metal railing and my feet touched down onto the field.

"Travis, what are you doing?" Mom screamed. "You can't go out there!"

I didn't even turn around. Instead, I picked a football up off the ground and waved for Carter to cut across the middle. He hesitated at first, then made the move. I reared back and fired him a perfect strike.

Next, Alex Moore, number eighty-eight, a pencil-thin sophomore with blazing speed, raised his hand for a long pass. He was one of the Gators' leading receivers. A few years back, I'd seen Alex play against Carter for Santa Fe High School, Beauchamp's biggest rival. Now Carter and him were roommates in the athletes' dorm.

I really launched one deep. For a second, I thought I'd put too much arc on the pass, overthrowing Alex. But he glided down the field like a gazelle and caught the ball in full stride.

I looked up and saw a uniformed security guard heading right for me. I froze in my tracks. Then, just as that security guard got within arm's reach of me, I heard Goddard's voice boom from off in the distance, "Leave him be! I'll handle this!"

Goddard's slow walk over to me was like torture. Carter looked concerned too—his entire upper body practically deflated.

"Big arm, Travis. That's how to lead a receiver," said Coach Goddard, behind a widening grin.

"Uhhh, thanks, Coach," was all I could get out of my mouth.

"I watched that game video you sent me, of you at quarterback," he said.

"You did? Really?"

I'd sent it almost four months back and hadn't heard a word. Mom told me Coach G. probably asked for it just to be polite. So I didn't get my hopes up about hearing anything back.

"I was impressed," he said, patting me on the shoulder. "You showed a lot of maturity and poise under pressure."

"Thanks," I replied.

Coach G. walked out to the middle of the field toward Carter, where they started to talk. Alex jogged over in my direction, flipping me the football and flashing a big smile.

"My brother's brother," he said, making a fist and then reaching out to bump his black knuckles against my white ones. "You can throw that pass even deeper next time. I had another gear left."

"I will," I replied, completing the fist bump. "Careful what you wish for, though. I can really let it fly."

"You see this number eighty-eight I wear? Laid out on its side, that's double-infinity," Alex said, leaning over nearly parallel to the ground, like he was diving to make a catch. "You can't overthrow double-infinity. It catches up to everything."

"Oh. O-*kay*," I said, a little confused as Alex loped away.

I was totally psyched about that praise from Coach G. But I began to stress, thinking Carter might be catching grief from Coach over me stepping onto the practice field. The two of them were far enough away that I couldn't hear a word. Still, Carter had a look on his face like he wasn't completely enjoying the conversation. So I dropped the football on the ground and headed back to the stands.

CARTER'S TAKE

Coach walked up to me, squaring his shoulders with mine. I was convinced that I was about to get screamed at for Travis jumping the fence and coming onto the field.

"How old's your brother again, Gardner?" Coach asked, as I removed my helmet.

"Nearly thirteen, Coach. He'll be starting the eighth grade in September," I answered, breathing a little easier. "Listen, I'm sorry Travis stepped—"

"He's sprouted up like a weed since I've seen him last, hasn't he?" Coach cut me off, looking back in Travis's direction. "How tall are you, Gardner? Six-five?"

"Maybe a shade under, if I get measured in my bare feet," I answered, clueless as to where the conversation was headed.

"He'll probably be even taller. You can tell by the size of his hands. Huge for a boy his age," said Coach.

I glanced down at my own hands for a moment and said, "I never noticed before."

"He's got a big chance at this game. Could be the best Gardner to ever play college ball," he said. My ears began to burn. "I'd love to have him here in five years."

The last thing I wanted to do was to look like I was hating on my own brother. But I couldn't listen to any more without saying something back.

"I mean, Travis is talented and all. He's the best quarterback his age in Alachua. But that's only out of about two or three hundred kids in his Pop Warner league."

"He has all the tools. All he needs to do is mature. You can be a real influence on him," Coach said, like Travis was *my* responsibility.

Somewhere in my head, I could hear Dad's voice giving me the same advice after the divorce.

Be sure to keep an eye on Travis. You're the man of the house now.

I felt a surge of frustration run through me.

"Sure, Coach. I'm on it," I said, squeezing the bars on my face mask until I thought they might snap.

"Good man, Gardner."

It was unbelievable. I hadn't played my first college game yet, and Coach thought Travis could be better than me. So why was I busting my butt in the weight room and staying up nights studying the playbook?

One of the assistants came over and told Coach that the team was ready for him.

"All right, let's get this season started!" Coach bellowed, before he blew his whistle. "Station drills!"

Meanwhile, Travis had climbed back into the stands, where Mom gave him a high five. The people seated in that section actually cheered for him.

I put my helmet back on and jogged over to the other tight ends, almost wishing that Coach had exploded at me.

CHAPTER 4

The next day, I was busy redecorating *my* bedroom, since Carter had started living on campus. Only, Mom wouldn't let me move his bed out.

"Your brother's just twenty minutes away. He'll be sleeping here a lot—on vacations, some weekends when football season's finished. Don't go overboard, okay?" she said.

"I'm not trying to evict him or anything," I told her. "I just never had a room of my own before. I really want to make it about *me*."

So I shoved Carter's bed as far into the corner as I could. Then I boxed up most of his football trophies and moved the rest of them behind mine on the top shelf of the bookcase. I heard the house phone ring and Mom pick it up in the kitchen. Then, after a few minutes, there was a knock on my door, along with a sharp bark. Mom stepped in, carefully cradling the phone while Galaxy jumped up beside her.

"Travis," she said, with a smile and a sort of stunned

look on her face, "this call's for you." She handed me the phone with her eyes on mine.

Dad only called my cell. And Mom wouldn't have talked to him for that long, not without an argument. I thought it might be that Lisa Marie Batelli, who'd been my partner for a school summer reading project. Mom insisted that she had a major crush on me.

"Hello," I said into the receiver, like I was walking into a room with the lights off.

"This is Head Coach Elvis Goddard, Travis. How are you today?"

"Fine, Coach. I'm fine," I said, as Mom's smile grew wider.

"I spoke briefly with your mother, and she said it was all right for me to make you this proposal. Travis, I'd like to offer you a football scholarship to play at Gainesville."

For a second, the only sensation I could feel was goose bumps popping up over my body. My mouth hung open and I couldn't speak.

"Travis?" said Coach G. "What do you think? Would you like to become part of our Gator family?"

The words rushed out of me in a flood of emotions.

"You bet, Coach. Yes! Yes! Yes!" I said, with my heart beating like a big bass drum in a halftime marching band: *Boom! Boom! Boom!*

"It's not official yet. It can't be. You're too young to commit to a college," Coach G. said. "This is just a personal promise from me to you that there'll be a place for you here in five years."

I turned to see Mom still standing in the doorway, looking as proud as could be.

"I won't let you down, Coach," I said. "You'll see. I'll do whatever it takes to make it."

"I know you will, son. That's why I'd only make someone like you this offer," he said, before clearing his throat. "Now, this proposed scholarship is highly unusual. Let's talk a little bit about the media. They should be calling soon."

* * *

I phoned Dad first with the news, even before I thought about calling Carter.

"You've reached Max Gardner of Nationwide Insurance, serving all of your insurance needs in Tarzana, Woodland Hills, Encino, Reseda, and the greater Los Angeles area. I'm serving a valued member of our Nationwide family right now, so leave a detailed message and I'll get back to you as soon as possible."

I hated that message. I'd heard it so many times over the past two years, I knew it by heart.

"Call me back right away. You're not going to believe it," I said.

Over the next five minutes, pacing around my bedroom, I broke my own rule and left Dad two more messages. So he'd know I was serious. I even thought about changing my phone message, just for him. Something like: *"This is Travis Gardner, the newest scholarship quarterback for the Fightin' Gators. I'm either being interviewed by the media or polishing up my passing game. I'll be sure to return your call when there's a break in my busy schedule."*

But I really wanted to tell Dad myself.

A few minutes after my last message, Dad called back. He started to give me grief about overloading his voicemail. But I cut him off quick.

"What do you think happened to *me* today?" I asked.

"I don't know, but you need to tell me in less than three minutes. I'm heading into an important sales meeting."

"Coach G. gave me an athletic scholarship!" I said, sitting on the edge of my bed and twirling a football in my left hand.

There was a long silence before Dad said in a sarcastic tone, "So you'll be going up against college players instead of eighth-graders."

"Not for *this* season," I said, slamming the football down against the meat of my thigh. "Five years from now."

"Come on, Travis. What's this about? I know Carter's been getting all the attention lately. But—"

"It's all true. I swear. Check out ESPN," I said. "They're going to do a phone interview with me soon."

I threatened to put Mom on the line to back me up on everything. That's when Dad sounded like he was finally starting to believe me.

"Gainesville's committing to *you*? A full athletic scholarship?"

"If I want it, it's mine. But I've already told Coach G. yes," I said, letting myself fall backward onto the bed.

"Travis, I'm really proud of you. I agree, grab it while it's being offered. It's so easy for a football player to have a bad season or get injured. This is like an insurance policy for your future. Something you can count on," Dad said, as my eyes studied every little crack in the ceiling over my head. "Is it binding on their part?"

"No, it's just Coach G.'s word."

"Hmm. Okay. Still, it gives you lots of cushion in case you struggle," said Dad.

Only, I wasn't thinking about any of that negative stuff. I just wanted a chance to play the position I loved—quarterback—at the highest level possible.

CHAPTER 5

A producer from ESPN called. She wanted me to use the landline in the kitchen and not my cell for the interview. So it would sound clearer. Galaxy wouldn't stop barking, though, and Mom had to drop him off at a neighbor's house for a while.

"Galaxy's probably as excited as us," I said, when she got back without him.

"Dogs are like that. Most animals are. They're extremely intuitive. They can sense things," Mom said. "I've read news stories where people's pets knew an earthquake or tsunami was going to hit, hours before anyone else."

Mom seemed anxious, waiting for that producer to call back.

"Aren't you nervous at all?" she asked. "Millions of people watch that network."

"Maybe just a little," I said, shuffling the salt and pepper shakers around the table. "But I don't see why I should be. The interview questions will be about football and me. Those are two subjects I know. It's not like schoolwork or taking a test, where I have to study to find the right answers."

* * *

Several minutes later: Travis is on the phone, sitting at the kitchen table. His mother stands beside him, pacing a bit. Her arms are folded in front of her, and she's having a hard time standing in one place.

Producer: Travis, just stay relaxed. Scott will be on live with you in a moment. We already have some facts on you from the Gainesville Gators' media department. When you answer Scott's questions, try to make it more like you're having a conversation with him. Avoid "yes" and "no" answers. Okay?

Travis: I got it.

Mom (whispering): Is it live?

Travis nods his head.

Mom mouths the words, *"My God!"*

After several seconds, Travis hears ESPN SportsCenter's theme music.

Scott: Welcome back to *SportsCenter.* I wonder how many viewers remember what they were doing the summer before they entered the eighth grade. Getting ready for a final year of middle school? Trying to talk your parents into adding an extra hour to your curfew? Well, Travis Gardner, a quarterback from Alachua, Florida, is now making plans to attend Gainesville University, where—in five years—he may be playing football, after verbally accepting an offer from famed coach Elvis Goddard. Scholarship promises like these aren't completely unheard of. Several pre–high school quarterbacks have received them in the past, such as Chris Leak and David Sills. But, Travis, what was your first reaction to that phone call?

Travis: Oh, I was in total shock. It was something I never expected when I woke up this morning. But I look at myself in the mirror now and I'm almost a Gator!

Scott: I'm told you'll play Pop Warner football again this coming season. And for our viewers who don't know, that's the equivalent of Little League baseball. Travis, how do you think players in that league will treat you?

Travis: They'll probably do a big celebration dance every time they sack me. I know I would. I'd say, "I just tackled the kid with the scholarship. Where's mine?"

Scott: I know it's been less than a day since you accepted the scholarship, Travis. But has it changed your life so far in any way?

Travis: Yeah, I'm on *SportsCenter* with you. That's amazing.

Scott (laughing): Glad we could be part of your special day. I'm sure our viewers are as well. But I have to ask you, Travis—and many people will wonder—is this too much, too soon, for someone your age to handle?

Travis: Well, it's always been my dream to play quarterback for the Gators, ever since I was young. And—

Scott: And just how *young* was that, Travis?

Travis: Maybe since I was nine or ten. If it wasn't the Gators, if it wasn't Coach G., I probably wouldn't have accepted. But this is a dream come true, a kind of destiny for me.

Scott: I understand you have an older brother, Carter, who's currently a freshman on the Gainesville football team.

Travis: Yes, sir. I hate to admit this, because we have a real rivalry going. But Carter's probably the reason I got the scholarship. It's made me a better player, training with him.

Scott: Sounds like you two have a strong relationship. Travis, you still have a long road ahead of you. There's a final year of middle school and then four years of high school before you reach your goal of playing football at Gainesville. What will you do to keep yourself on track over that time?

Travis: I'll keep working on my game, trying to improve. I'm going to spend a lot of time in the weight room getting stronger. And just try to be a better recruit, not to disappoint Coach Goddard. He really believes in me.

Scott: I think I can speak for our viewers as well when I say that I'm rooting for you, Travis. In five years, I hope to see you lead the Gators onto the field in Gainesville. Enjoy the journey, my young friend.

Travis: Thanks. I'll try my best.

Travis hangs up the phone.

Mom (softly): Yaaaay!

Mom smothers Travis with a hug.

* * *

Right after my interview on *ESPN*, Dad called back.

"I just want to make sure you realize what you've been handed here," he said. "That you're ready for this and willing to work hard."

"Don't worry, I am," I told him. "Coach G. knows what he's looking for in a prospect. He really sees something in me, like maybe I was born to do this."

"You still need to make a realistic plan," he said. "You'll have to take stock of where you're headed, make yourself a workable map to get there."

"I've got Mom and *you* to help out with that," I told him. "All I have to concentrate on is football. That's just fun to me. I can't think of anything I want to do more."

For something like an hour, we talked about how my interview had gone, about playing quarterback, and about my future. It felt like every second of that conversation was about us. It felt like he was really *Dad* again, not somebody who had an obligation to call. Like he didn't have a job that was more important than me, or another family. There wasn't a single word about swim meets or problems over me being a lefty. And even though I knew he was calling from California, I almost let myself believe he'd be coming home that night.

CARTER'S TAKE

I was sitting in a meeting room with the rest of our receivers, waiting for the coaches to arrive. The seniors had been giving me a ton of static for refusing to carry their shoulder pads to practice. But I didn't care about any freshman tradition. I was here to be a football player, not a pack mule.

"You still got a lot to learn," whispered Alex from the seat next to mine. "Remember, you're a freshman. When one of these seniors tells you to carry their pads, you do it. No questions asked. And you better smile about it. Or else a dozen of them will jump you after practice and duct-tape you to a goal post."

"I'm not bowing down to anybody whose job I'm trying to take," I said.

"There's a big difference between how you can act on the field and off it. Between the white lines, yeah, rock 'em. Hit 'em in the mouth," said Alex. "But for now, before you've even played a single game as a Gator, in the dorm, on the sidelines, and in meetings—you're the low man. It'll be over after this season. I went through it, same as you. Your turn will come. That's the natural order of things."

"I'm tired of waiting my turn. Seems like there's always somebody ahead of me who shouldn't be. I want to make sure things are different here."

"You're my roommate. That means I'm responsible for you, to teach you how it goes. Don't embarrass me—especially with both of us being from Alachua. Being roommates, that's supposed to make us closer than brothers on this team."

"Yeah? What's *closer* than brothers?" I asked.

I already knew Alex was an only child. That it was just him and his mother.

"I don't have any blood brothers. But I've got more than one hundred football brothers on this team. I've got their backs and they've got mine. Inside of that circle, there's family." Alex interlocked his fingers. "Maybe one day I won't just call you brother. I'll call you *fam*. But that's still a ways off. Something you've got to earn."

Coach Harkey came into the meeting room and walked up to me.

"Hey, Gardner, I'll need your brother's cell phone number."

"Uh, sure, Coach," I answered, reaching into my sweats for my phone, while my brain tried to make sense of his request. "Why?"

"I want to start him off on a proper conditioning

program," answered Harkey. "It's going to be easy for him to think he has to overdo it."

"Overdo what?"

"Haven't you heard? Coach Goddard offered him a scholarship about an hour ago."

"What? Is this some kind of joke?" I asked, shooting Alex a quick look and watching for his expression. I figured those seniors were messing around with me for not carrying their shoulder pads to practice.

"No joke, Gardner. He's the newest Gator—five years down the line. It's already been reported in most of the media outlets. Now, have you got that number for me or what?" Harkey asked.

"You mean this is for *real*?"

"I'm way too busy to play games," Harkey said as he copied the number off my phone.

Soon as Harkey left, the seniors in the room let the disses fly.

"Gardner made such a bad impression, Coach G. went to Pop Warner to replace him."

"We should make him carry his little brother's shoulder pads."

I said to Alex, "This is completely insane."

"Why? Sounds exactly like what you were asking for," Alex replied. "You're not the low man anymore. You got your baby brother beneath you."

"Or way over me," I said, before I stood up and left to call Mom.

CHAPTER 6

Carter found out about my scholarship before I could tell him. He called Mom to talk about it. Then, after a while, she handed off the phone to me.

"Hey, bro, you coming to live here in the athletes' dorm? I'm looking for somebody to wash my underwear," Carter said.

"Sorry, it's gonna be five years. Maybe you'll learn how to do them yourself by then," I said, loving every word of it.

"How's it feel?" he asked.

"You know the feeling. Great. Just great."

"Technically, we won't be teammates. I'll graduate before you ever get here."

"Then I'll have to meet up with you in the pros," I said. "Throw my first NFL touchdown pass your way."

"I wouldn't be against that."

"Oh, and remember, I won," I told him.

"Won what?"

"The race to be on *SportsCenter.*"

"I guess that one's yours," he said. "You have the Powerball numbers for tonight, lucky bro? I hear it's up to twenty-five mil."

"How about our uniform numbers? Twelve for me. Eighty-five for you. How many more do you need?"

"Forget it. You might have used up your luck for a lifetime," he said. "Anyway, I'll see you for dinner tomorrow tonight."

"Dinner?" I asked.

"It's Mom's idea. She'll tell you," Carter said. "Seriously, though—good going today. If you need any advice on becoming a Gator, I'll be here for you."

"Thanks. I really appreciate it."

"And listen, if it rains, make sure to stay inside. The way you've been beating the odds lately, you might get struck by lightning."

"Ha, ha. That's *so* funny."

* * *

The news about my scholarship spread fast. Starting at around four o'clock, kids and neighbors from around my way were knocking at our front door, wanting to congratulate me. Guys on my Pop Warner team, including Damon, kept stopping by, one after another. I invited them all inside to see my new room. Then Mom decided to make a run to the supermarket for soda and chips, and the party was on.

"I can't believe this is happening to somebody *I* know," said Damon. "Yesterday, you were just a regular kid, like the rest of us."

"I still am," I said. "I just know where I'm playing college football."

"Yeah, but that's so huge," he said. A bunch of other guys nodded. "It's like you don't have to worry anymore. That's your Willy Wonka Golden Ticket right there."

All I knew for sure was that I was totally stoked and wanted a football in my hands more than anything. I organized a game of touch in the street outside my house. There were seven of us, so we played three-on-three, and I was all-time QB for both sides.

My left arm was feeling like fourteen-karat gold. I must have thrown five straight touchdowns. In one play, I even told somebody to make his cut between a pair of parked cars. I stood there with total confidence and laid the ball perfectly between a black Lincoln and a silver SUV. I spiraled it maybe four inches over the Lincoln's roof rack, right into my receiver's hands.

My phone kept interrupting the game. It was going off nonstop with calls and texts from kids I knew at school. After a while, I let most of the calls go straight to message or answered their texts with a Quicktext reply: *Thnx, won't let U dwn.*

Only, I made sure to answer the text from Lyn Wilson differently. Lyn was Damon's twin sister, although they didn't look anything alike. She was one of the cutest girls at Westside Middle School and the star pitcher on the girls' softball team. Damon had clued me in that she'd mentioned my name a few times. So a couple of months ago, I asked Lyn out for pizza. She didn't say no, but she didn't say yes either. She just sort of changed the subject without ever giving me an answer. That left me feeling like an idiot.

Her text read: *congrats on d ftbll scholarship! dats amazn! btw i lk xtra cheez on my <).*

Lyn's real first name was Marilyn. That's why she only had one N at the end. I'd heard her pitch a real fit once about teachers and coaches who'd spell it L-y-n-n.

I replied back: *lyN, i lk xtra cheez 2 n h8 peppa. ltz gt 2gtha sn.*

I decided to forget about what happened the last time. I was riding so high right then, nothing could make me feel bad about myself.

* * *

The next night, Mom took me to Wok N Roll, my favorite Chinese buffet, to celebrate. Carter and Alex met us in the parking lot there. Carter didn't have a car of his own. Mom didn't have the money to buy him one and pay the insurance. But Alex drove a brand-new blue Mustang convertible.

Carter made the introductions: "Mom, you know Alex, my roommate and *new chauffeur.*"

"Pleased to meet you," Mom said. "I'm glad *you've* got that job tonight. I've been driving Carter around way too long."

"Well, I don't work cheap. He's buying my dinner," said Alex. "But I really wanted to get to know our youngest brother here. Welcome to the Gators, Travis."

Alex extended a fist to me.

"Now that you're one of us, let me show you how we do it proper on this team. It's called a Gator Pound," he said.

First, we did a double fist bump. Then he opened his hand wide like the jaws of a gator and swallowed my hand up, before I did the same to his.

"Hey, how come *I* don't know that yet?" asked Carter.

"Don't worry, I'll teach it to you," I told him.

I ran my hand over the warm hood of Alex's car.

"Wow, I'd love to be seen in this instead of our old Toyota," I said.

"It's a beauty," Mom added. "How can your parents afford it for you?"

"It's just my mama and me, and she can't. She's struggling for money like everybody else. She manages a sub sandwich shop off South Main," said Alex, twirling his car keys around his finger one time before they disappeared into his palm. "But I've got some *extended family* that helps me out."

"Is that the fam you were talking about?" Carter asked him.

"No, they're not that kind of close," Alex answered. "They just got some extra bucks to burn."

"Well, it's still *very* nice of them," Mom said, as we headed toward the restaurant.

Once we got seated at a table and the waiter brought our drinks, Mom said there should be a toast in my honor.

"Carter, why don't you make it," she said.

A look of pain came over Carter's face, like somebody was twisting his arm.

"All right," he said, and then raised his sweetened iced tea.

I lifted my black-cherry soda and held it over the middle of the table.

"What can I say about Travis?" Carter started off. "He's talented, hard-working, and—except for Alex here—the only one I know with as much passion for football as me. I'm proud to call him my brother."

I loved what he'd said, and we all touched glasses with a clink. Then I filled my plate from the buffet with General Tso's chicken, Chinese spare ribs, and pork fried rice. I made three separate trips, coming back with the same things every time.

"Travis, why don't try something new?" asked Mom.

"Because I know what I like," I answered.

"Maybe you just *like* what you *know*," said Alex.

"Are you studying philosophy?" Mom asked him.

"Communications," answered Alex, who'd finished off a huge plate of crab legs. "Maybe after playing in the pros, I'll be a broadcaster."

Alex and me were almost the same size. He was just a half-inch taller and probably ten pounds heavier.

"Excuse me for saying this, Alex," Mom said. "But you don't really look like a college football player."

"Yeah, I get that a lot," said Alex. "Maybe too much."

"He's thin, but he's fast. Real fast," said Carter.

"Not thin. *Lean*," Alex replied. "I'm trying hard to put on another fifteen pounds of muscle. Then maybe turn pro after this season."

"If you want to put on weight, forget the crab legs," Carter said, turning a fork through a tall mound of pork lo mein. "You need more meat and pasta."

"Leave school? What about your degree?" Mom asked.

"If he turns pro, he doesn't need a degree," I said. "He can hire someone with a diploma to count all his money."

Mom slapped at my wrist with her chopsticks for saying that.

"I gave my mama my word I'd graduate, no matter what," said Alex. "I don't break those kinds of promises. So if leave for the NFL, I'll go back to school during the off-season to finish up my BA."

I snuck a quick look at my phone after the buzz of another congratulations text.

"Since when are you good with phones out at dinner?" Carter asked Mom.

"It's Travis's party," she answered, giving me a sideways glance. "He's entitled to be rude to his guests if he wants."

"Okay, I'll put it away," I said, sliding the phone down into my back pocket.

As soon as I did, a kid who played Pop Warner football came up to our table with his father standing behind him.

"You're Travis, right?" he asked. "You got the college scholarship yesterday."

He wanted my autograph. It was my very first one. I almost couldn't believe it. There wasn't any paper around. So the waiter brought me over a blank dinner bill, and I signed that.

My hands were shaking a little. I tried to sign my name as neat and straight as possible. But after I'd finished, I saw the letters were slanting slightly downhill. The kid was thrilled to have it anyway. Then Mom introduced everyone at the table.

The father recognized Alex's name and made a fuss. That's when the kid asked for Alex's autograph too. In the middle of all that, the waiter brought our check, and I noticed Carter slip Mom some money for Alex's meal. As we stood up to leave, the owner of the restaurant came over. The waiter told him something in Chinese, and then the owner shook my hand with a big smile on his face. He asked me to pose for a photo with him.

"For our wall of stars," he said, pointing to some celebrity photos behind the cash register.

"Sure," I said. "No problem."

Mom took the photo for him as Carter and Alex stepped outside, then went to pay the check before I went outside too. I was hoping Alex might let me sit behind the wheel of his Mustang for a minute. Carter and Alex hadn't gone that far yet. They were standing by the restaurant while Carter broke into his fortune cookie.

"What's it say?" I asked him.

"Nothing," Carter said, staring at the small strip of paper like he'd been cheated.

"What do you mean, nothing?" asked Alex.

"Here, look," said Carter, showing us the paper.

It read: *THE FORTUNE YOU SEEK IS IN ANOTHER COOKIE.*

Alex and me both laughed hysterically and even traded a Gator Pound over it. Then Mom walked out and handed Carter back his money.

"What's this for?" Carter asked.

"The owner wouldn't take anything from me," she answered, snapping closed her purse. "He said that it was his treat."

"Mom, I don't think we can do that," Carter said. "We're on scholarship. We're not supposed to accept gifts for being on the team. That's an NCAA rule, a big one."

"Should I go back inside?" asked Mom.

"Hey, your brother's not on scholarship yet, right? It was his party. Your mom's not on scholarship either, and she was the one trying to pay," said Alex. "Take my advice. Just keep on walking."

THE GAINESVILLE SENTINEL

Section D/Sports – Columnists

GATORS ROBBING THE CRADLE?

KAREN WOLFENDALE

Yesterday, Coach Elvis Goddard made headlines by offering a football scholarship to incoming eighth-grader Travis Gardner of Alachua County. Of course, that story of a local boy who dreamed of quarterbacking his hometown Fightin' Gators will appeal to the public far more than the other news the football program has been making recently.

Two weeks ago, the NCAA announced a preliminary investigation into claims made by a pair of former Gators. These players contend that during their time at Gainesville University, they received illegal cash payments in the form of "money handshakes" from boosters seeking to reward them for their good play. So Coach

Goddard's sudden offer to a fresh-faced youngster—and the change in the conversation about Gators football that comes with it—shouldn't be completely shocking.

"Travis visited our first practice this summer. I was impressed with his size, raw talent, and enthusiasm," said Coach Goddard. "By making this offer now, I wanted Travis to know he'd caught my eye. And that in the future, he'll have a home at Gainesville."

According to NCAA rules, a prospective student-athlete can't sign an official letter of intent until late in his junior year of high school. So the offer is not binding for either party at present. The scholarship is just talk, which restricts the NCAA's jurisdiction over it. However, the offer will undoubtedly have an effect on Travis Gardner and his family as they move forward. Over the course of this season, and the years to come, this column will periodically report on Travis's life as he inches closer to his goal of becoming the Gators' starting quarterback.

Coach Goddard has six years remaining on his current contract.

"If I wasn't committed to being here in the future, I wouldn't have offered this scholarship," said Coach Goddard. "I wouldn't invite Travis to join our Gator family without me being around to guide him."

CHAPTER 7

The Saturday after I started the eighth grade was huge. My first Pop Warner game since the scholarship started at 8 a.m. Carter's first college game with the Gators was that afternoon at one. I might have had three hours' sleep on Friday night, thinking about it all. Earlier that day, I'd gotten a call from the sports media department at Gainesville.

"Coach Goddard asked us to set you up a Twitter account," the voice said. "He doesn't allow his current players to tweet, but you're a special situation. Starting tomorrow, he wants you to tell people what's going on in your life. You know, all of the good things—the hard work, the excitement. You just text your thoughts to us. We'll read through them, make sure they're appropriate, and then we'll post for you."

"Do you think I'll have any followers?" I asked.

"Don't worry. Coach is completely behind this," answered the voice. "We'll publicize it on our website, on campus, and push it in media outlets throughout Florida and nationally. Your story is of great interest to many people, Travis. We're going to make sure that number only gets bigger."

"What'll I call myself?"

"We already have a username for you. It's *TravisG_Gator*."

Right from the start, I liked the sound of it.

* * *

Saturday morning at the field was crazy. Mom sat in the first row of the bleachers, surrounded by six or seven reporters. A crowd of more than five hundred showed up. It was the most people I'd ever played in front of. And every one of them seemed to know my name.

"Go get 'em, Travis! This is the start of something special!"

"Travis, show us that Gator spirit!"

Cameras pointed at me from every angle. There's no press section at Pop Warner games. So those reporters were practically spilling over our sideline.

"Yo, Trav, you're making us all into rock stars," said my center, Damon, who'd snap me the football. "Maybe I'll get the next scholarship someplace."

"I'd like that. It'd mean nobody could get past *you* to sack *me*," I told him.

Damon stood only five-nine but weighed nearly a hundred and ninety pounds. He was huge—without much muscle tone. Over the summer, he'd picked up the nickname Ground Round because he won a hamburger-eating contest, chomping his way through fifteen burgers in just twelve minutes.

His sister Lyn came to see us play that Saturday too. Our pizza date had been great. I had even worked up the nerve to kiss her by the end of it. My first *real* kiss. When it was over, I felt like spiking a football and doing a celebration dance.

Lyn could have been our prettiest cheerleader. I'd asked her on our date why she didn't go out for the squad.

"I'd rather be playing than cheering," she answered. "Some guys don't like that. They're probably afraid of getting beat by a girl."

I knew Lyn was right, because I certainly didn't want to be in the batter's box against one of her windmill fastballs.

Butterflies did cartwheels inside my stomach as I jogged onto the field. I stepped up to the line of scrimmage and barked out signals.

"Thirty! Blue, eighteen! Blue, eighteen! Hut, hut!"

Damon snapped the ball into my hands, and I found the leather laces. All of that nervousness disappeared. I was where I belonged. Where I was most comfortable. And I just played football.

On my first pass of the game, I had a receiver a full step behind the defense. I never hesitated. The football glided out of my left hand and spiraled down the field. I threw an absolute laser beam, and the ball stuck inside my receiver's palms.

That easy groove stayed with me. I sensed every bit of defensive pressure coming my way. I wasn't thinking—I was reacting. I noticed a defender being a real ball hawk, looking to jump every route our receivers ran. He wanted to get there a step early and intercept one of my passes. So I took a snap and purposely kept my eyes glued to the receiver he was covering, making that defender believe the ball was coming his way. Then I gave the perfect pump-fake. That ball hawk bit. He jumped the route, nearly springing out of his cleats. Only, my receiver kept right on running vertically.

The defender slapped his hands against his helmet, knowing he'd been suckered. Then I floated the ball to my wide-open receiver, giving the ball hawk even more time to think about what had just happened.

For the rest of that game, I had one eye on the clock, wishing it could slow down. I wanted to stay on that field forever. The game felt more like one big party being thrown in my honor.

When it was over, I grabbed my phone to text the media department my first official tweet. As I typed out the message, Lyn patted me on the shoulder pads, congratulating me. The cheerleaders had gathered around me too, along with a bunch of reporters waiting to ask questions.

@TravisG_Gator *Won 35–14. Receivers played great. O-line protected me 2 the max. No dirt on my uni. Mom won't even have 2 wash it. Go Gators!*

Two hours later, I had put on a Gators T-shirt and was standing inside *their* locker room beside Carter. Coach G. had invited me to run onto the field with the team for their first game of the season, then watch from the sidelines. Except for Alex, I was much smaller than everyone there to begin with. But in their pads and helmets, the players seemed even bigger.

"So, you ready?" I asked Carter, who was sitting on a three-legged stool in front of his locker. "Because I am."

"I'm glad *you're* ready. All you've got to do is run through the tunnel and not fall on your face," he said. "I've got fifty plays running through my head and a checklist of key words to remember for audibles at the line of scrimmage."

"Tell me the keys. I'll quiz you," I said.

"Can't. I'm not supposed to tell anyone who's not part of our offense," he said, smearing eye-black across the bridge of his nose and beneath his eyes until he looked like a raccoon. "We're keeping the circle closed. So our signals don't get out by accident."

"You think I know players on Florida International?" I said, annoyed. "How am I going to give any secrets away?"

"Sorry, bro, I don't need to get called out by any of the coaches over doing something stupid."

A few seconds after that, Alex came over and asked Carter, "You know what to do when our QB shouts, 'Hero'?"

"Yeah, I know," answered Carter.

"Let me hear," Alex said.

Carter mouthed, *Go pattern*, like I couldn't read lips. I felt like some second cousin visiting from out of town instead of his brother.

Then Coach Goddard stepped into the center of the locker room, and everything went silent for his pregame speech.

"If you've been listening to the sportscasters, you know we're thirty-one-and-a-half-point favorites today. That extra half-point always makes me laugh. Maybe it's because those Florida International boys have to come to our home, to our swamps. What are they, the Panthers? A swamp's no place for kitty cats. It's Gator territory," he said with a half-smile. "But when you run out onto the field, I can guarantee you that scoreboard's going to read zero-zero. That gives those boys all the chance in the world to beat you. Nobody gives you anything on the football field. You have to take it. You have to step up and perform. Now, go out there and play like Gators! Be champions!"

An electric current shot through the locker room, like Coach G. had hit some secret switch. I could feel the spark starting in the soles of my feet, running all the way up my spine. I went charging toward the door along with everyone else, with Carter already far ahead of me.

CARTER'S TAKE

Standing inside that dark tunnel, waiting to run out onto the field as a Gator for the first time, was the most incredible feeling in the world. My teammates and I were squeezed so tight, we practically stood on top of each other in our cleats. No one could keep his feet still.

Up ahead, in a glimpse of sunlight, I could see a row of huge, pointed teeth. They belonged to a thirty-foot inflatable gator covering the outer mouth of the tunnel.

"Make way for Coach G.!" a voice shouted from the back of the line. "Everybody, slide left!"

I felt the crush of my teammates as we hugged the tunnel wall. Then, as Coach G. strode past, I actually trembled a little bit.

A moment later, I could hear the theme music from *Jaws—Bump, bump, bump, bump. Bump, bump, bump, bump.*

I'd been to enough games as a fan to know that the Jumbotron was playing a clip of a gator moving through a grassy swamp toward its helpless prey.

Then Coach G. screamed, "That's our cue! Gators, let's move! Go! Go!"

I charged through the tunnel toward the bright light, onto the field, to the sound of that cheering crowd.

Turning back around, near the end of the line, I saw Travis pass beneath that same row of teeth. Coach G. put a hand on the back of his neck and guided my brother over to the sideline as photographers snapped their photo.

I tried not to let it get to me. I really did. But I couldn't help what I was feeling. I needed to go out and make *my* mark. I needed to become a big-time college football stud. Not the brother of the kid who got the scholarship.

CHAPTER 8

For most of the game, I stood on the sideline next to Carter. Only, he'd walk away every time a photographer or TV camera came anywhere near us. Carter got on the field for just three offensive plays, without making a catch. The quarterback didn't even throw the football in his direction. But Alex caught seven passes and scored two touchdowns.

On one of those scores, Alex was running full speed along the sideline. A defender had a perfect angle on him, ready to shove him out of bounds. But just as the defender got there, Alex threw on the brakes. He moved like a Ferrari in reverse, going from sixty to zero in a split second. That defender ran right past Alex without ever touching him. Then Alex accelerated again, out-running the rest of the Panther defense to the end zone. His celebration dance lit up the Jumbotron as Alex spun the football on its end and pretended to warm his hands over it, like it was a roaring fire.

I tried to joke with Carter that his uniform had

stayed as clean as mine was after my Pop Warner game. Only, he didn't come close to smiling.

In the locker room after the game, Coach G. was all over the team for every little mistake they'd made.

"Sloppy, egotistical, and a total lack of commitment!" he ranted. "That's what struck me the most about our play today!"

Somebody walking into that locker room, who hadn't seen the game, probably would have thought the Gators lost 47–0 instead of winning by that score.

THE GAINESVILLE SENTINEL

Section D/Sports – Columnists

TOP PROSPECT

KAREN WOLFENDALE

This is the first in a series of articles looking at the life of top football prospect Travis Gardner as he begins his five-year trek from Westside Middle School to a football scholarship at Gainesville University.

After scrimmaging with the snooze alarm on his clock radio, Travis Gardner drags himself out of bed. It is 6:40 a.m. Still in his pajamas, Travis places both his palms flat against the chilly hardwood floor, preparing to knock out a set of twenty-five pushups.

Since August, when Coach Elvis Goddard offered him a football scholarship, Travis has pushed himself to do six such sets a day in order to build more muscle.

From down the hallway echoes the voice of his mother: "Don't lose track of time! Oatmeal or cold cereal for breakfast?"

66

"Cap'n Crunch! No milk!" Travis answers between pushups six and seven.

Travis has exactly forty-four minutes before the school bus arrives. If he isn't waiting on the street corner opposite his modest single-story house, the driver will leave without him—football scholarship or not.

He has already had to make the nearly two-mile walk once this semester.

After Travis's seventeenth pushup, Galaxy, the family's black Labrador retriever, interrupts the set, begging for attention.

"That's eight pushups I have to make up later," Travis says, scratching the streak of white fur on the dog's chest.

Despite the sudden fame that has come with his scholarship, Travis's life isn't so different from that of other eighth graders. Friends, school, and Pop Warner football all make demands on his time. Of course, he also has nearly 200,000 Twitter followers as @TravisG_Gator. And on the bus ride to Westside Middle School in Alachua, Travis is the only student with a reporter riding shotgun.

"Other kids look at me like I've made it. Lots of people do. I don't want to let any of them down," said Travis. "Sometimes it's a lot of pressure."

It isn't all a world of worries for Travis, who sports an off-the-charts "cool" factor normally reserved for teenage pop stars.

"Everybody wants me to sit with them in the cafeteria. So I've been spreading myself around, sitting at three or four different tables a week," said Travis. "Other kids want to help me with my homework now too. That's good, because it leaves me extra time to train. My mom's even excused me from some of my house chores. That way I can concentrate more on football."

Travis's older brother, Gainesville University freshman Carter Gardner, plays tight end for the Fightin' Gators. His scholarship offer came late in his senior year at Beauchamp High School.

"I got here the hard way, living in the weight room and running extra pass patterns by myself in the backyard," Carter said after a recent Gator practice. "But I think it's great that Coach sees something special in my brother."

Has the publicity surrounding Travis distracted Carter as he tries to establish himself as a college player?

"People ask me things like, 'Aren't you the brother of that kid who got a scholarship?'" said Carter, who has not caught a pass in his first three games with the Gators. "I usually joke around and say, 'That's me, just keeping a space warm for him until he gets here.' But I'm really focused on my own college football career."

Travis's Pop Warner team has won its first three games this season. He has also thrown nine touchdown passes against only two interceptions. Yet reservations about Travis's scholarship still exist, as well as charges that the offer lends the Gator program positive publicity in the face of an NCAA investigation. Under the condition of anonymity, an opposing Pop Warner coach spoke to the *Sentinel* about these allegations.

"There's no doubt Travis is the best quarterback in our league, really advanced for his age. But a scholarship to someplace as competitive as Gainesville? This early? Elvis Goddard is ten times the coach I'll ever be. Who am I to second-guess him?" the coach stated. "But I do."

A sea of students parts in front of Travis as he makes his way from the curb to the green cinderblock Westside Middle School building. His classmates meet him with cheers of encouragement and high fives.

"Way to go, Travis!"

"Rock that interview!"

At the school's doors, an assistant principal dutifully checks students' ID cards as they enter the building. Travis strolls past without having to produce his. Another perk of his newfound celebrity.

CHAPTER 9

I got invited to seven Halloween parties. That had to be some kind of eighth-grade record. Only, I didn't get to enjoy it for long, because Mom made me turn most of those invitations down.

"How come I don't get to decide for myself which parties I'm going to? They're *my* invitations, not yours," I argued.

"Travis, if I haven't met the parents, the answer's an automatic no," she said. "And I'm not a car service. I'm not going to be driving you from house to house. I think two parties in one evening's a good limit for you."

I wanted to argue about it more. But whenever Mom pulled that *I'm not a car service* line, I knew she'd heard enough. I didn't need to tick her off. The last thing I wanted to do on Halloween night was to take the bus, or walk and have kids think I was out trick-or-treating.

I came up with the idea for my costume watching a horror movie on cable. I smeared fake blood on an old, deflated football before cutting it in two with a pair of garden sheers. Then I had Mom sew one half of the football to the front of my jersey, and the other half to the back, like it had knifed completely through my chest.

"There, that's a sight I hope I never live to see," she said, pulling the last stitch tight as I modeled the jersey.

"Don't be silly, I'm the quarterback," I said, looking at myself in a full-length mirror. "I'm the one who fires the football."

Kids loved my costume and made a fuss over it all Halloween night. First, I went to Patty Young's party, where half of my Pop Warner team was hanging. Five or six cheerleaders kissed me hello on the cheek. I spent most of the time pretending I could dance and playing drums in *Rock Band* for a while. When it was time to leave for Damon and Lyn's, I didn't even think about wiping off the lipstick marks from those cheerleaders. I figured it added to my costume. But I guess Lyn, who was decked out as a cowgirl, didn't agree.

"Travis, exactly what kind of *games* did they play at that other party?" she asked at the door. "We have *Wii Sports* and *Just Dance* here. But that might be a little tame for you."

Later on, Damon told me that somebody had texted Lyn a picture of those cheerleaders kissing me.

"Who? Haters?" I asked Damon.

"Did you think *everybody* was a fan of yours?"

The rest of that night, Lyn played me pretty cold. I couldn't get her alone to talk even once. I had a bigger problem, though. The report card for my first marking period was coming out in a couple of days. The deal Mom always had with me was that I needed a B average to keep playing football. She'd actually pulled the plug on my season two years ago, when my average slipped down to a C-minus. I'd just gotten blasted on both my math and science quizzes. So I was already planning damage control.

* * *

The next day, while the two of us were eating dinner, I told Mom, "You know, teachers purposely don't give high grades at the start of the semester. They don't want you to get a swelled head, thinking you know everything already."

"I can see how that might stop you from getting straight As for now, not Bs," she said, stabbing her meatloaf with a fork.

"Well, it's the same principle," I said, pushing my peas behind the mashed potatoes, like they were the walls of a fort. "If you really deserve a B, you might get a C-plus. Just to keep you hitting the books."

"Are you getting all Cs?" she asked.

"No, I don't *think* so," I answered. "But if I were, how would it look to Coach G. if you didn't let me play football this year? It could cost me my scholarship."

"Travis, if you don't get good grades, you won't get into college. There'll *be* no scholarship."

"I'm not failing or anything. There's been a lot of distractions this semester. It's harder than you could imagine."

Mom paused for a second.

Then, with a hint of sympathy, she said, "I've thought about that, how all of this attention might affect your grades."

"I just need a little cushion."

"I suppose," she said. "We'll see what your report card looks like when it comes out. Then I'll decide."

When dinner was done, I took all the dishes to the sink without being asked and started to scrub them.

* * *

My first-marking-period average turned out to be a B-minus. In the end, Mom was happy with that. So was I, because I felt like I'd won something from her that I could use in the future, in case my grades *really* took a hit.

* * *

"Guess what? I'll be in Florida late tonight," Dad said. I'd just gotten out of school on Friday when he called.

"I made reservations a few minutes ago. I'll meet you at your game tomorrow morning. Then we'll drive down to Disney, come back Sunday night, and I'll fly out first thing Monday. So get all of your homework done *pronto*."

"Really? You're coming here? One-hundred-percent sure?"

"I'm packing a bag right now," Dad said.

"You know Carter's in Arkansas," I told him. "The Gators are playing the Razorbacks there tomorrow night."

"I could only juggle my schedule so much. It had to be this weekend for me," Dad said. "Just be ready with everything *you* need to do. Oh, and I'm not flying across three time zones to see you lose a football game."

"You show up, and I'll guarantee a win," I said.

The next morning, Mom dropped me off at the field with my travel bag. Only, she wouldn't drive away until she actually saw Dad standing there.

Dad wrapped his arms around my shoulder pads and gave me a hug. "I can't believe that's you, Travis. You look like a college football star already. You've grown up almost overnight."

"You think so?" I asked, as Dad took the bag from my hand, leaving me with just my helmet to carry.

"I sure do," Dad answered. He leaned in close to me and said, in almost a whisper, "Travis, there isn't another player here with his future mapped out the way yours is. That's special."

Dad had brought his video camera to record the game, to show everyone he knew back in California what I could do. My left arm had nearly doubled in strength since the last time Dad saw me play. Still, I felt really anxious about it, like I had something to prove to him. As I took my first snap, I forgot all about my mechanics, and my opening throw sailed a foot over the receiver's head, incomplete.

"That's on me," I told my teammates coming back to the huddle. "It won't happen again."

Calling signals at the line of scrimmage, I was thinking about my next pass, figuring how to adjust my release. Then I took the snap from Damon. Almost everything was perfect on the play. The protection, the route the receiver ran—I even had a clear alley to throw. But I overcompensated. The ball felt awful coming off my fingertips and handcuffed my receiver at his knees, falling incomplete again. I kicked at the ground, launching a clod of turf through the air, cleaner than any pass I'd thrown so far.

Eventually, our defense got me a turnover close to the other team's goal line. I walked back onto the field, concentrating on what Coach G. had preached to me in the backyard: *calmness and execution.* So I cleared my mind and let my muscle memory take over. That's when my passing game finally started to click. I called a fade route for the left corner of the end zone, near where Dad was standing with his camera.

"Shiner sixty! Shiner sixty!" I barked. "Hut, hut!"

I took a quick one-step drop. Then I lofted the ball high into the air. After reaching the peak of its arc, the football floated down like a feather, over the outstretched arms of the defender, and into my receiver's hands. Just like playing lawn darts as a kid against Carter and Dad.

I raced into the corner of the end zone with both hands high over my head, signaling a touchdown. That throw took a lot of the pressure off me. Afterward, I settled down and passed the ball with much more accuracy. It wasn't close to being my best game of the season. And I knew every mistake I'd made was captured on Dad's video. But we got the victory I'd guaranteed him, 23–14.

@TravisG_Gator *New TV ad? Travis, you just won your 4th straight game. What are you going 2 do now? I'm driving to Disney World with my dad!*

Dad rented a red two-seater Corvette. The drive from Alachua to Orlando is a little more than a hundred and twenty miles, and on the way down there, Carter called my phone.

"I saw your tweet," Carter said. "Are you with Dad?"

"Yeah, he's here. We're heading to Disney right now. I'll put you on speaker."

"Saw your brother play quarterback this morning," Dad said, resting one hand on the steering wheel and the other on the stick shift. "It was a bit of a struggle. But he got it done with that left arm of his."

"When did you guys plan *this*?" asked Carter.

"Listen, it's all on me that it happened while you're on the road," Dad said. "My schedule broke just right yesterday, and I jumped on a plane. I'll be back to catch one of your home games soon. I promise."

"Whatever," said Carter. I could hear him exhaling into his phone. "All right, I need to go get ready for tonight."

"We're going to watch it on TV. It's on ESPN, I think," Dad added.

"Be sure to take Travis on that Mission: Space ride. Maybe he'll puke his guts up again."

"I was ten back then," I said, as we zipped past another road sign. "I'll give your best to Minnie Mouse. I hear she likes guys with big ears."

Carter disconnected after that.

* * *

First thing at Disney, Dad and me hit the Magic Kingdom. There were long lines everywhere, but we waited it out to ride Splash Mountain and Space Mountain. Then we did my favorite, the Haunted Mansion, with the stretching room, the creepy wallpaper with the watching eyes, and the portrait of the young guy who turns into a skeleton right in front of you. After that, we went over to Epcot. We tried Soarin', where you're suspended above the floor on a fake hang glider. There's a big movie screen in front of you, and they do all kinds of things to fool your senses so you feel like you're really flying. Dad got excited when we soared over a bunch of California sites, like the Golden Gate Bridge and the beach at Malibu.

"That's how beautiful the Pacific Ocean is," Dad said. "Look, that's LA. I can almost see my house."

I loved it. But it was kind of sad too, knowing Dad shared all of those places for real with a teenage stepson and not me.

We were starving afterward and had an early dinner at a Mexican villa. I stuffed myself full of tacos and burritos until I practically belched refried beans. Then we left the park and checked into our hotel room. Dad sat down by the flat-screen to watch Carter's game, which was already halfway through the first quarter, while I took a quick shower. A few minutes later, I stepped out of the bathroom, still towel-drying my hair. Coach G.'s face filled the screen as he jawed from the Gators' sideline with a referee.

"What's *he* like?" asked Dad.

"Who, Coach?"

I thought about it as the damp towel worked my brain.

"He's like a football Zeus," I answered, sitting down on the edge of one of the two beds in the small room.

"He snaps his fingers and things happen. Lightning bolts, earthquakes—"

"Scholarships," said Dad, completing the list.

"Yeah, those too."

Then I asked if Carter had been in the game yet.

"One of the senior tight ends turned an ankle," Dad said. "Carter's been in a few plays already."

"Really? You should have called me out of the shower," I said. "Did he get his first catch?"

"Not yet," he answered.

Five minutes after that, Carter *did* make his first catch as a Gator. Even watching on TV, I saw the pass pattern developing. As the quarterback released the football, I could almost feel it leaving my own hand on a straight line to Carter. And I felt the same way watching the replay. Dad and me exchanged high fives. But that was just the start of us celebrating. Before the game was over, Carter made three more receptions, one of them for a twenty-six-yard touchdown that put the Gators ahead for good in the fourth quarter. When Carter scored, our screams were so loud we could have drowned out that whole Country Bear Jamboree back at the Magic Kingdom. Me and Dad jumped up and down in each other's arms, while, in that Arkansas end zone, Carter and Alex did exactly the same thing.

CARTER'S TAKE

Almost two hours after our win, I was still walking on air. My first catch and touchdown. Alex had to steer me through the crowd in our hotel lobby. The place was mobbed with our fans, and I felt like I could finally hold my head up high and get the respect I deserved.

"So where are we headed?" I asked Alex.

"Now that you're a superstar, at least for one game, there's somebody here who wants to meet you," he answered, while I waved to a group of Gator fans who'd actually recognized me.

"Yeah, who?"

"My extended family, the filthy rich one. You'll know the dude as soon as you see him, from his car commercials. Mr. Walter Henry."

"You mean the guy at Gainesville Motors? The one dressed like Indiana Jones, whose car tosses him a bull whip and pulls him out of a snake pit?"

"That's him," Alex said, as we took a sharp turn into the hotel's restaurant, and then walked right past a sign that read: *PLEASE WAIT TO BE SEATED*. "He's a Gaines-ville alum. Flew something like twenty people here as his guests to see the game."

Alex headed straight for a private room in the back. As soon as we walked in, Walter Henry, who sat at the head of several long tables pushed together, stood up to greet us. He was probably in his late thirties, built like an athlete himself, with wide shoulders.

Walter Henry shook Alex's hand first. Then he reached out for mine and said, "Carter, what a pleasure to finally meet you. The two of you—great game, and a satisfying night for Gator fans."

Henry turned to his guests and said, "Everyone, this is Alex Moore. You'll see him play in the NFL soon, I'm sure. And this is Carter Gardner, who caught that big touchdown for us tonight. They're two of the reasons we're celebrating."

One of his guests asked me, "Isn't your kid brother the one with the scholarship?"

I nodded my head, feeling the weight of those words.

"I hope he can play as well as you did tonight," said a second guest.

"Yeah, me too," I said, beginning to smile.

"Please, join us for something to eat," said Walter Henry, snapping his fingers for a waiter. "Menus. Two more chairs."

"No, we can't stay but a minute," said Alex. "Coach has a team curfew for us. We're flying out early tomorrow morning. I just wanted to pay my respects and introduce you to Carter."

"Enough said," Walter Henry replied, walking us toward the door. "You know, I'm from Alachua as well, Carter. Just like you and Alex. Born and raised."

"Really? Where?" I asked.

"I grew up on Fifty-Third Terrace," he answered. "Went to Beauchamp High too. Played football for a while, before I turned to running track. Liked fast things— that's how I became interested in cars. Then a business degree from Gainesville made me a success. That's why I like to give back, donate my time and resources to the university, especially the football program. My customers are Gator-crazy. Most of the people around this table represent my larger accounts. Say, Carter, what kind of car do you drive?"

Alex was almost snickering as he said, "Go on. Tell him, Mr. Hitch-a-Ride."

"I don't have any wheels right now, sir," I answered, embarrassed. "It's a money situation with my family."

"First of all, call me Walter," he said. "Lots of young people are financially challenged. I get it. You're busy being a football player and a student. Sometime soon, why don't you come down to my dealership? Maybe I'll have a model there that you can afford?"

"Sure, I'll do that," I said. "Thanks, Walter."

"Don't mention it," he said, reaching into the front pocket of his trousers. "We boys from Alachua have to stick together, help support one another. And, Carter, when you come to see me, if your brother Travis is free, bring him along."

"All right," I said, as Walter shook my hand good-bye.

Right away, something felt different. But I didn't want to make any kind of scene.

"Carter knows. Everybody wants to meet the kid," Alex said.

"Hey, he could be our future," Walter said as we left. "Go Gators."

I waited until we were outside the restaurant before I looked into the palm of my hand.

"Alex, there's four one-hundred-dollar bills here," I whispered as if we'd just robbed a bank.

"Then you must have outplayed me tonight. I only got three," he replied.

"What should I do?" I asked.

"I can't be your conscience," answered Alex. "I'm just showing you the ropes, how the game gets played. You read the papers. You know about the investigations. Maybe a third of our team has hookups like this. Some better, some not. It's on you now. Nothing's stopping you from turning around and giving Walter back his cash. But if isn't you, he'll bless somebody else with it. So make up your mind."

CHAPTER 10

My Pop Warner team ended the season undefeated. That put us into the regional playoffs, with a home game against the top team from Tallahassee. We played in a driving rainstorm, making it almost impossible to pass. I had a receiver wide open on a curl route, coming back to me. So I set my feet in the slop to throw. An instant after I released the ball, a huge gust of wind came up. The football flew fifteen feet over my receiver's head, spinning end over end like a kite without a tail in a hurricane. Even when the wind wasn't gusting, the rain kept the ball so slick I could barely control it.

We fumbled the ball away three times. My stomach began to ache. I hadn't lost a single game since getting the scholarship from Coach G. That was something I desperately wanted to hold on to.

I barked at the running back, who'd had two of those fumbles. "Get a grip—on the ball and yourself! This is the playoffs! It's win or go home!"

Despite all the turnovers, we were trailing only 10 to 6 entering the final two minutes of the fourth quarter. With the ball in my hands, I decided if I couldn't pass, I'd use my legs. So I dropped back and then scrambled outside the pocket with the ball. I saw a lane and sprinted along the edge of the sideline. Rain dripped down my face mask and into my eyes. It was like running blind on a greased railing. The opposing D finally forced me out of bounds at the Tallahassee eight-yard line. That gave us a first down with 1:07 left on the clock, with the other team out of timeouts.

Inside our huddle, Damon, covered in mud from head to toe, said, "If we take two or three plays to punch this ball in, they won't have any time for a comeback."

"That's the plan," I said, before calling my own uniform number. "Twelve blast, quarterback keeper."

I clapped my hands together, breaking the huddle. Then I approached the line and stood over Damon as he got ready to snap me the ball.

"Blue thirty-two! Blue thirty-two!" I shouted, trying to make the defense think I'd pitch the ball to the Alachua running back wearing that number. "Hut!"

I'm not sure what happened next. Maybe Damon got nervous and snapped the ball too soon, or maybe I pulled my hands away before I got a good grip. But the ball squirted loose. I dove to the ground, desperate to recover it. Only, it bounced off somebody's foot, disappearing beneath a pile of players. A kid from Tallahassee came out of the pile holding the ball high, like a mud-covered trophy. Then *they* ran out the clock on *us*.

After the game, Damon took all the blame himself.

"I'm a moron! A fat idiot!" he said, almost in tears as he pounded his helmet against our bench. "I was too quick on the snap! I threw away our whole season!"

I thought hard about taking some of the heat. But there were two reporters hanging around, waiting to talk to me. I knew those reporters wouldn't mention Damon. He was just another kid on the football field. *I* was the one they were there to write about. And I didn't want to chance Coach G. reading anything negative about me.

"It happens. Just another mistake in a sloppy game," I told Damon, trying to console him. "We'll do better when we play for Beauchamp next year."

"That doesn't change how I let *this* team down," he said, hanging his head.

I heard some other players popping off, saying things like, "Ground Round really killed us" and "Maybe his mind was on his next hamburger."

So I had to figure Damon heard them too. I didn't see Damon pick his head up for a while after that. Deep down, I felt awful about not stepping up to at least share in the blame.

@TravisG_Gator *Lost today. Rain killed our passing game. Props to ALL my teammates! Great season! Next stop BHS!*

A few days later, Mom took Carter car shopping, and my brother asked me to tag along. We went down to Gainesville Motors. Alex came with us too. He was tight with the owner of the place, Walter Henry, who I'd seen in a bunch of my favorite TV commercials, playing everybody from Honest Abe Lincoln to Luke Skywalker in *Car Wars*. Turns outs Walter grew up playing football in Alachua, and he couldn't wait for me to throw him some passes in the lot out back.

"I'm sure we'll find a car for Carter today. I've got plenty of good deals for Gators and their families," said Walter, who caught almost every ball I threw his way. "But I'm also hoping I can interest Carter and Travis in doing some part-time work for me, like Alex does sometimes."

"I'm interested," I said, thinking about finally having some money of my own. "What would I do, wash cars?"

"No, nothing like that. Not for you, Travis," Walter answered, tucking the ball beneath his arm and bringing us all into a huddle. "You could help *sell* cars."

"An eighth-grade car salesman?" Mom asked.

"Not *exactly* a salesman," said Walter. "I picture Travis greeting potential buyers. Just being himself. Being that kid who was offered a football scholarship because he's got big talent. The same talent we're known for here at Gainesville Motors."

"I'll have to give it some real thought," Mom said. "Travis has had a lot to handle this year. This may interfere with his studies."

"Of course, you're the final word," Walter told Mom. "Maybe we could try it out a few Saturdays."

"Please, Mom. My football season's already over, so I've got more free time," I said. "And it'd mean less money you'd have to give me for stuff."

"We'll see," she said. "It might be all right to *try*."

I exchanged a high five with Walter, just to hold him to his part of the deal.

Carter didn't seem to care one way or another about me *or* him working there. His only interest was getting himself a car. And he did, after Walter's top salesman gave Mom a special price on a two-year-old silver Malibu. Carter even chipped in. I'd never known my brother to be quiet about money, but I guess he had some secret savings to use.

* * *

I thought the Gators had a great regular season, finishing with a record of ten wins and two losses. But Coach G. was unholy mad with the team for losing a game late in the season, costing them any chance to play for the National Championship.

"I promise you this," Coach G. steamed after that loss. "You're all going to watch that title game together, to see what you threw away. I don't care how painful it is. Then, when you see what you've lost as a team, you might want it bad enough next year."

Being second-best wasn't anywhere in Coach G.'s mind-set. And I wanted to think that way too. The Gators had almost six weeks off before going down to Miami to play Maryland in the Orange Bowl on New Year's Day.

With my season finished, I started some unofficial training on Sunday mornings at the football complex with Carter, Alex, and Coach Harkey. I'd take the city bus down to the complex. Afterward, Carter would drive me home. I was glad to have that ride. Because the way Coach Harkey would push us through those workouts, I'd be too sore to walk to the bus stop, even with the slack he'd cut me.

"You're still maturing. I expect everybody else here to push it past the limits of exhaustion," Harkey told me on the first day of workouts as I tightened the laces on my sneakers. "When you feel like you're about to puke, back off. No matter what your mind tells you about wanting to compete, your body might not be ready."

That sign with the raised letters read BLOOD, SWEAT, AND TEARS. It didn't mention anything about puking. I figured Harkey had to be joking. But he wasn't.

For exercise one, we jumped up onto a wooden box from a standing start, then back down to the floor. Over and over, with a timer set for two minutes. The height of the box was adjustable. I had mine set at almost two feet, the same as Carter. I started out nice and easy, finding a good rhythm. After a while, though, leaving the floor got harder, and my thighs began to burn.

When the timer finally buzzed, I stopped, resting my hands on my knees and taking deep breaths.

"Travis, that first buzzer means there's thirty seconds left," said Carter, who was still jumping. "You're supposed to really push now."

But I could only get off one more jump.

Alex had his box set six inches higher than ours, and he made it look easy. At the next buzzer, I tried to jump up onto his box and nearly fell flat on my face.

After a half-minute rest, Harkey had us doing military-style pull-ups.

"Head up, back straight!" he hollered. I struggled on the bar, with my arms beginning to burn as much as my thighs.

When that was done, we sprinted forty yards at full speed across an indoor turf mat.

"Jog, don't walk!" Harkey yelled, as I headed back to the starting line.

Next came squats at a weight station.

"You're going to get bigger! Stronger! Faster!" Harkey snapped at everyone. "Remember, it may be your body on the line, but it's *my* reputation!"

We did that full circuit of exercises three straight times. I didn't puke, but I came close. So I decided never to eat breakfast again before one of Harkey's workouts.

CARTER'S TAKE

I was driving Travis home after the second of Coach Harkey's Sunday workouts. Alex came along for the ride. We were more than halfway there when Alex said, "Take a left turn and then a right up at the next traffic light. There's something I want to show you."

Those directions took us to South Main.

"Park in the space out front. Ignore the signs. They don't give tickets on Sundays around here," Alex said as we pulled up to the sub shop his mama managed.

"Are we eating?" asked Travis. "Because I didn't bring any money."

"This is my place, my treat," said Alex.

A little bell rang as Alex opened the shop's front door.

"Look out, Mama. I brought two hungry boys with me who never tasted subs as good as yours before," Alex said.

The shop was long and narrow, with six or seven empty tables running from one end of it to the other.

"My baby!" she called out. "Come here and give me some sugar!"

Alex's mama was short and a little older than I'd imagined, with a streak of gray running through her brown, curly hair. Her son nearly vaulted the counter to give her a big kiss on the cheek.

"Are these some of your football brothers?" she asked, looking us over.

"These two are practically fam," Alex answered. "This is my roommate, Carter, and his bro, Travis."

"Oh, well, one of you is famous in this store," she said, pointing up at the big menu on the wall over the counter.

I scanned the menu, reading off the selections until my mind stopped cold.

"Carter, look! There's a sub named after me—a Travis G. Gator!" Travis shouted excitedly. "It's got pepperoni, provolone cheese, spicy mustard, and dill pickle slices."

"It's one of our best sellers," Alex's mama said as she put on a pair of clear plastic gloves.

"I don't know," I said. "Any sandwich named after my brother should be stuffed with baloney."

Alex had a grin on his face a mile wide over my reaction—and Travis's.

"I've got to try one," Travis said.

"So, Mama, that'll be one Travis G. Gator, one Alex Po' Boy—"

"There's a sub named after you too?" I asked.

"For almost two years now—lean turkey and Swiss on a club roll," answered Alex. "Don't sweat it. Score a few more touchdowns, there might be one named after you."

"Is that how Travis got his?" I asked.

I ordered a sub with ham and American cheese. But I'd just about lost my appetite. Then the three of us squeezed in around one of those little tables after Alex's mom handed us our orders.

"Come on, Carter. Try some of my sub," said Travis. "It's really good."

I didn't want to, but I could see how thrilled Travis was. In my heart, I knew that none of this was his fault, all of the attention he'd been getting. And it was partly my job to help Travis grow up. So I took a gut check, put whatever jealousy I'd been feeling aside, and took a bite of his sub.

CHAPTER 11

That January, Mom and me drove to Miami to see Gainesville play Maryland in the Orange Bowl. And I had so much access to the team that Mom started calling me "the Gators' unofficial mascot."

I was standing on the sideline with the score tied 7 to 7 and less than one minute remaining in the first half. That's when Coach G. called for a wide-receiver screen pass.

The play put Alex split out wide to the right, on the tight-end side. At the snap, he faked running downfield and stayed at the line of scrimmage. The quarterback delivered him the ball on his numbers. The rest was up to Alex and his flying feet.

He nearly juked the first defender out of the guy's socks, losing him fast.

A second defender had a clear shot at Alex. He was about to make the tackle when Carter threw the block of his life. You could hear the *huhh* of air leaving that defender's lungs as Carter flattened him like a pancake.

Then Alex sprinted into the clear and didn't slow down until he was five yards past the goal line. The stadium's video screen played Carter's block back from two different angles.

"Thank you, fam. That touchdown's part yours," Alex told Carter at halftime, wrapping his arms around him. Then Alex called out to everyone in the locker room, "Did you see that monster block? Fam went *bam!*"

All that smiling and laughing didn't last long, though. On the second half's first play from scrimmage, Alex caught a cleat in the turf while he was making a sharp cut. His left knee twisted with a ton of torque, buckling beneath him. He fell to the field screaming in pain, with both hands clamped around his knee.

The trainers had to lift Alex up and carry him to the sideline.

"Looks like he tore something," I heard Harkey tell Coach G. after talking to the trainers. "Could be serious."

Within a few minutes, Alex was sitting on the back of a cart with his legs stretched out in front of him. A white towel hung over his head as he rode back to the locker room, but I could still see the tears running down his eye-black and onto his cheeks. Alex slammed the cart's metal railing so hard I thought he might have broken his hand.

"Wide receivers, it's next man up!" Harkey hollered toward the bench.

That's something football coaches say—*next man up.*
It means the team can't worry about missing any one
player. That somebody needs to step up and take his
spot, almost like he was never there. To prove it, the
Gators' quarterback, Billy Nelson, fired a second-half
touchdown to Alex's replacement, securing the victory.
Before the game was over, Alex came back out onto the
sideline on crutches.

"What'd the doc say?' Carter asked him.

"Can't see ligaments on an X-ray. I'll get an MRI
tomorrow. They think it's my ACL, maybe torn. If it is,
surgery. Six to eight months minimum to recover," Alex
said. "Guess I'm out of the NFL draft. No pro team's
going to take a chance on damaged goods. I'll have to
come back and play another year, to show I still got my
speed."

Carter shook his head. "Too bad. I was looking forward to breaking in a new roommate."

"That's your miserable luck, huh?" Alex replied.

✦ ✦ ✦

From mid-January until June, I worked most Saturdays
at Walter Henry's dealership. That meant I had my own
money for things like pizza and movies. By the end of
March, Lyn got over being mad, and I took her out a
few more times. I liked Lyn a lot. But I liked all the
attention I was getting from other girls too. That's why,

for the eighth-grade dance at the end of the school year, I didn't ask any one girl to go. Instead, I went with a bunch of friends, guys and girls, and we danced together that night in a big group.

Dad didn't fly to Florida for my middle-school graduation. He said it was less of a graduation and more of a moving-up ceremony. He was probably right. We were talking twice a week then, mostly about how long I'd stay at Gainesville U before I left for the pros. Dad *did* send me a $200 check as a present. Thanks to Coach G.'s scholarship, Mom let me spend it all on video games instead of putting it into my college fund.

CHAPTER 12

Throughout the summer before ninth grade, I stayed focused on sharpening my quarterback skills by running every drill imaginable—for footwork, arm strength, and accuracy.

Three times a week, Carter and Alex, who was still rehabbing his left knee after ACL surgery, would run pass patterns with me doing the throwing. Harkey added an extra day to our off-season training schedule and had us working out at the football complex on Sundays *and* Wednesdays. Alex outworked everybody else. Only, his knee was still healing slower than he wanted.

"Six to eight months' recovery—that's what it's supposed to be. But that's for anybody, not an NFL-caliber athlete," said Alex, lying on the complex floor. He flexed his knee, using a giant rubber band that stretched from his hands to the sole of his foot. "It's been nearly six months already. I've got a season to play soon. I can't make the sharp cuts I need to. There's no explosion in my first step."

"Patience, bro. It'll come. Just keep pushing. That's all you can do," said Carter, mid–butterfly stretch. "Any way you look at it, you're still two steps faster than me."

"You're a tank. I'm a Ferrari," Alex said. "You see Travis overthrow me by five yards on that deep ball yesterday? How'd that ever happen?"

"Because my arm's getting a lot stronger," I said, straightening my legs after my own butterfly stretch.

"Yeah, I forgot," grumbled Alex, releasing the rubber band with a snap.

As Alex stood up, Harkey came over and put an arm around his shoulder. "Don't sweat it, Moore. I'm personally going to get you there. No matter what I have to do. No matter what *you* have to do."

Harkey walked Alex over into a small office for a private conversation, closing the door behind them.

"What do you think Harkey's telling him?" I asked Carter.

"I don't know. But if anybody can get Alex back to one hundred percent, it's Harkey and Coach G.," Carter said, rising to his feet and twisting the cap off a fresh bottle of Gatorade.

* * *

A few days later, Alex was in a slightly better mood. Between him and Carter running routes, I must have thrown them almost a hundred balls. After lunch at the sub shop, they drove me home, and I challenged Alex, who'd been bragging about his video game *skillz*, to *NCAA Football* on my Xbox 360.

Galaxy went out of his mind when he saw Alex. He was jumping up and down, shaking his rubber ball with the bell inside. It was all Alex could do to get past Galaxy to my bedroom, so he tossed the ball down the hallway, taking advantage of the clear path while Galaxy went to fetch it.

Me and Alex sat down on the edge of my bed, facing the TV. We both wanted to play as the Gators.

"Sorry, it's my game," I said. "*My* choice."

"That's such kid nonsense. 'My game.'"

"What'd you expect? He *is* a kid," said Carter from his bed in the far corner of the room.

"Not anymore. I got a college scholarship and a job."

"All right, I'll be Alabama," Alex said grudgingly.

The players on the screen looked exactly like the stars from the real teams. They even wore the same uniform numbers and had the same moves.

"Think you'll be able to cover yourself in this game?" Carter asked Alex.

"Nobody can stop double-infinity—not even me," he answered. "Do they have a player who looks like you? Number eighty-five?"

As Carter shook his head no, Alex jabbed him a little more. "Too bad, I was going to leave him completely uncovered. Nobody would be throwing to him anyway."

"I would. First off, he's my brother. Second, you're leaving him open," I said, as Alex kicked off to start the game.

Two minutes into the first quarter, my phone rang.

"Carter, here, check this," I said, taking one hand off the controller just long enough to toss him the phone.

"It's Dad," he said, checking the display.

"Answer it," I told him.

"He's calling *you*, not *me*," said Carter.

"You gonna play your pops cold like that?" asked Alex, setting his defense for another play. "I wish mine could be on the line. I'd pick up in a heartbeat, no matter what."

"He died?" I asked Alex.

"From diabetes, when I was ten. That's something I got shortchanged on. I love my mama, but a dude only gets one pops," Alex said.

The phone stopped ringing. Dad's call went to message before Carter flipped the phone back onto my bed.

A minute later, I sent Alex's avatar streaking down the field. It caught a long pass and out-sprinted three Alabama defenders into the end zone. That avatar even copied Alex's touchdown dance, spinning the ball on its end and then warming his hands over it.

Alex exploded. "You win! I'm out of here!" He stood up and bolted for the door. "Even my Xbox character's faster than me now."

I'd never seen Alex lose his temper like that. I figured it was from all the pressure he was feeling, trying to get his knee healthy again.

"Where you going? I'll drive you," said Carter, getting up too.

"Back to campus. I need to talk to Harkey. Do some extra rehabbing."

* * *

High school started for me in the last week of July—not classes, but football practice. It was ninety-five degrees that first day. Coach Pisano stood on the field in front of eighty players, ready to give a speech. We were broiling beneath the sun in our football pads, while Pisano wore a tank top, shorts, and sneakers with no socks. He had a tattoo of a pouncing bobcat that started on his right anklebone and ran up his calf. Pisano had coached the Beauchamp Bobcats for close to twenty years, and even played for them when he was in high school.

Coach Pisano cleared his throat. "Ahem."

That's when some senior players took their cleats to the butts of a few freshmen who were stupid enough to be sitting on the ground. The freshmen stood up in a hurry. Carter had played four years for Pisano. He'd clued me in to what was coming. So I'd been on my feet all along. I had let Damon in on it too. And he wore a big grin, since some of those freshmen were the ones who'd talked trash about him after that botched snap in our last Pop Warner game.

"A commitment, that's what I'm looking for. Not just a commitment to be here, to take part. But a commitment to give it your all. A sacrifice. Maybe some of you don't know what that means. Well, I'll spell it out for you. This morning I had bacon and eggs for breakfast. The chicken that gave up those eggs probably thought it had made a sacrifice. I don't. Not compared to the pig that supplied the bacon. That's what I'm looking for from all of you. If you can't give it to me, if you're just here to be seen wearing the uniform, leave now."

Everybody's eyes seemed to search the crowd. But nobody walked away.

"Good," said Pisano. "Then let's play Bobcat football."

Last season's starting quarterback had graduated. Now the Bobcats had only two quarterbacks with any kind of experience: me and a junior named Aiden Conroy. Aiden was warming up on the sideline, throwing to one of the receivers. He stood an inch taller than me, with wider shoulders. He sported freckles, short red hair, and a strong right arm.

I walked up to him to say hello, but he waved me off with a shake of his head.

"I already know who you are, scholarship boy. But

this is *my* team. I put in two years here as backup QB. It's my turn to be top dog. So get used to sitting on the bench and carrying my jockstrap."

Halfway through his rant, I was ready to clock him. Only, I was afraid of breaking my hand on his jaw and missing the season. Some upperclassmen who'd heard Aiden's comments were laughing out loud. I figured if that's what they respected—a smart mouth—I'd come right back at him.

"Maybe I'll let you carry *my* jockstrap. *Before* I wash it."

That got some reaction from the upperclassmen too. Only, none of it was positive.

"Freshman better learn his place."

"Thinks he's got mad swag."

Aiden glared at me and spit out of the corner of his mouth. None of the receivers offered to warm me up. I guess they'd already picked a side. So I called Damon over and started playing catch with him to get my left arm loose. I stood just a few feet from Aiden, to let him know I wasn't going anywhere.

I'd only seen Damon a handful of times over the summer. We'd mostly kept in touch by texting. By my third toss to him, I noticed he had lost a lot of weight, maybe twenty pounds.

"You on Weight Watchers or something?" I asked before zipping him a pass. "Offensive linemen are supposed to pack on pounds, not take them off."

"Got tired of being a blimp," Damon said. "If I have to change positions, so what? I feel better this way."

"What else can you play?" I asked.

"Not sure," he answered. "Wherever I can help out."

Aiden piped in, calling out to Damon, "Hey, maybe you can be our new backup quarterback. I hear that job's still wide open."

That's when Pisano walked over, ending all the talk. He set up quarterback drills, with both me and Aiden throwing to the receivers, tight ends, and running backs. Pisano had us splitting an equal number of reps, and I could tell Aiden was annoyed.

After twenty minutes, if I had to be totally honest, I thought Aiden's throws were sharper than mine. Aiden must have thought he'd outplayed me too. Because at the end of that first practice, he shot me a grin like any competition between us was over.

I barely got any sleep that night. I was imagining the headlines—*TOP PROSPECT RIDES BENCH AS SECOND STRINGER*. Doubt crept into my mind. Aiden couldn't beat out last season's quarterback, a guy who'd lost as many games as he'd won. How could Aiden possibly look better than me?

I was surprised, on the second day, when Pisano gave me *more* reps than Aiden. He had me throwing on the side to some of the starters. And I could feel the pressure to be perfect beginning to build inside of me with every pass.

Sunday was our off day. But I didn't need any rest. I was looking for every edge I could get. So I went down to the Gator complex to lift weights and throw some more.

Amazingly, Alex's knee had recovered nearly one hundred percent. His quick first step was back. He flew down the field, cutting to the left and to the right at tight angles. And I couldn't overthrow him on deep balls, no matter how hard I tried.

"You look like that Alex Moore from the video game," I said, walking off the field with him and Carter.

"Double-infinity is back," said Alex, brimming with energy. "Know what? I'll do the driving today. I got myself a fast car for a reason."

So Alex and Carter took me home in Alex's Mustang convertible. Alex put the top down and zipped around Alachua like there wasn't any speed limit. As we drove up to our house, I spotted Mom planting flowers in the front yard. Galaxy was out there too, rolling in the grass with his ball.

"Hey, want to see something faster than you?" I teased Alex, as we got out of the car.

I picked up Galaxy's ball. With the dog on my heels, barking for me to throw it, I walked into the street.

"Watch out for cars from these driveways," Mom warned me. "I don't need another vet bill."

When I hurled the ball down the block, Galaxy took off like a shot, running it down before the second manhole cover.

"How do you like the stride on him?" I asked Alex.

Once Galaxy came back, Alex lifted his knees up to his chest a few times and said, "Nobody's outrunning me today, two legs or four. Throw it again."

Carter tried to talk him out of it, but Alex wouldn't listen.

"Don't hurt yourself," warned Carter.

"Fam, please," Alex replied.

Then he looked to me, like I'd be insulting him if didn't do my part. So I cocked my arm and let the ball fly.

Alex exploded down the street, two strides ahead of Galaxy. He kept the advantage for the first fifteen yards or so, with his arms pumping hard and his footsteps beating a rhythm on the blacktop. Then, as Galaxy cut that lead in half, Alex's legs went into overdrive. An instant before Galaxy looked like he'd pass him, Alex reached out and snatched the ball from the air.

On the way back, Alex flipped the ball to Galaxy, who looked happy just to be playing.

"Now you know what fast is," Alex told me.

"All right, I can't watch that and not work on my speed," said Carter, hanging his head. "I'm running five sets of wind sprints right now."

"I'm down," Alex said. "I got plenty of gas left."

"Not me," I said, heading toward the house. "I'm ready for a nap."

"Finally, somebody's showing some good sense," said Mom, digging another hole for the last of her flowers.

When I reached our front door, I turned around and saw Carter and Alex at the far end of the street. They were walking back after their first sprint with Galaxy beside them, still carrying the ball in his mouth.

CARTER'S TAKE

Alex and I had just finished our first wind sprint when his face turned stone serious.

"I've never been too good at keeping secrets," he said, as I tried to catch my breath. "And I've got one that's burning up inside of me right now."

"You know me. I don't talk."

"This is really hard," he said, then gave Galaxy a quick scruff behind the ear. Hesitating, maybe.

I figured he needed to unload something about his mama—maybe it was her health, or maybe, God forbid, somebody from the NCAA heard about Walter's money.

"See how my knee's come together over the last couple of weeks? Well, I've been doing something more than rehabbing," he said.

We began to walk, still about thirty yards from my house, with Mom smoothing out the dirt around her flower bed.

"Like what?" I asked.

Coming to a stop in the street, Alex answered, "I've been juicing."

"PEDs?" I craned my neck to see that no one else was in earshot. "What for? You were working like an animal to get back."

"Just wasn't healing fast enough. I got too much at stake," Alex said.

He yanked the ball from Galaxy's mouth and tossed it for the dog to retrieve.

"I need to set this season on fire," Alex continued. "Get myself in position for the draft. An injury like this could cost me millions."

I almost couldn't believe what was coming out of Alex's mouth.

"What if you get caught, test positive? It could cost you everything."

"That's not going to happen," he said. "What I'm using is undetectable. Brand-new."

Galaxy came running back to me with the ball, all excited and jumping at my midsection.

"Where'd you even get something like that?" I asked, grabbing Galaxy by his collar to calm him down.

"Can't say."

"You might get a tumor from taking that garbage," I said, turning Galaxy loose. "I even heard it could stop you from having kids."

"I'm not going to be on it forever," said Alex. "Another cycle or two, tops. Just long enough to make an impression on those pro scouts. Let 'em see I didn't lose a step."

I still hated everything about it.

"So I've got your word on this, fam?" he asked.

I didn't want to, but I nodded my head.

"I'll take it to the grave," I told him, bumping my fist on his.

THE GAINESVILLE SENTINEL

Section D/Sports – Columnists

GATORS HOPING TO NAME THEIR PUNISHMENT

KAREN WOLFENDALE

According to NCAA officials, the hands of a few Gainesville University student-athletes may have been caught in the cookie jar. Head Coach Elvis Goddard contends that the allegations against these players in no way reflect the culture of his team.

Last spring, the NCAA launched an inquiry into alleged violations by members of the Gainesville football program. The investigation focused on players' receipt of "money handshakes" from boosters. At a press conference on Wednesday, Goddard and other members of the Gainesville athletic department announced they had finished an internal inquiry into the matter.

"Any problems here are individual ones, where individual athletes may have decided to accept something extra from a willing booster," Goddard said. "We've uncovered two instances where players may have been overpaid for their work as busboys at a charity dinner, and one instance where a player may have received too big of a discount on a flat-screen TV. We've reported this to the NCAA, and we're going to penalize ourselves for these possible transgressions by young people who are bound to make mistakes along the way."

By staying out in front of the investigation and naming their own punishment, the Fightin' Gators hope to avoid stiffer NCAA sanctions, which could include a bowl game suspension that would cost the university a chance at another National Championship and millions in revenue.

The Gainesville football program will reduce its number of scholarships from 85 to 83 over the next three years. The Gators will also hold two fewer practices per year during this period.

"I don't know what happens when other men shake hands. I only know what happens when I shake your hand," Goddard told reporters.

"We believe the NCAA will ultimately agree with us and accept these self-imposed penalties," the coach continued. "We've also written letters asking a pair of boosters, one who runs a local catering hall and another who owns an appliance store, to stay away from our program."

Now that Coach Goddard has put the cookie jar on the top shelf, we'll see if any resourceful "young people" find a kitchen chair on which to stand.

CHAPTER 13

Two weeks before the Bobcats' first game of the season, and one week before classes at Beauchamp started, Coach Pisano made his decision on a starting quarterback.

"Aiden! Travis! My office, five minutes!" Pisano shouted after blowing the whistle to end practice.

His voice shook me, even though I was standing twenty yards away. Realizing Pisano had said Aiden's name ahead of mine shook me even further.

Everybody on the team knew what that meeting was about. The handful of players who supported me, including Damon, slapped me on the back as I headed toward the locker room. The landslide of guys who were pulling for Aiden did the same to him, creating a sound like a steady drumbeat.

I didn't stop to take off my jersey or pads in the locker room, just changed my cleats for sneakers and then headed out into the hall. I took the long way around, walking almost the entire main floor to Pisano's office. When I got there, Aiden was already waiting outside the open door. Only, Pisano hadn't arrived yet. It was just the two of us.

"You going to tweet about this? How *I* got the starting job?" Aiden asked, dressed in black shorts and a gold T-shirt that read *Beauchamp Varsity Football.*

"The only reason I tweet is because Coach G. wants me to," I answered, like I was trying to hold Aiden off in a blocking drill.

"Yeah, Coach Goddard. He's the only reason we're standing here," Aiden said. "If he didn't give you that fake scholarship, there's no question I'd be the starter. You know that, right?"

Aiden was staring me down, waiting for an answer, when I heard Pisano coming down the hall. He was barking at an assistant coach over something that had happened at practice.

I hesitated, letting Pisano's voice get louder and closer.

"Go deal with it. Right now. And I do mean *deal* with it. I won't waste practice time on it again," Pisano told his assistant before turning his attention to us. "Step inside, boys."

Pisano didn't sit behind his desk. Instead, he sat on top of it, with his bare legs dangling off the front. I was too nervous to look him in the face. So my eyes dropped down, settling on his bobcat tattoo.

"Quarterback's always a difficult decision to make," Pisano said. "I'm a firm believer that a team needs a leader at that position, one clear starter to shoulder the load."

I was completely ready for Pisano to pick Aiden. I even pushed my toes into the floor, bracing for it.

That's when Pisano said, "Travis, you're going to lead the Bobcats this season."

I looked up to see his finger pointing right at me. I was so psyched. Something inside me wanted to grab one of the footballs on the floor of Pisano's office, just to feel it inside my hands.

I'd nearly forgotten Aiden was standing there until Pisano said his name.

"Aiden, you've earned a lot of respect from your teammates," he said. "The way to keep that respect and build on it is to accept this. To help Travis get up to speed with all of the details he needs to learn about our system."

"Sure, Coach," Aiden said, with his voice breaking just a bit. "Whatever the team needs."

Then Aiden stuck out his hand to me and I shook it. Standing there in my shoulder pads and jersey, with the starting job mine, I suddenly felt twice his size.

@TravisG_Gator *Bcame the Bobcats starting QB 2day. So grateful. It was a great competition. Now I'm #ready2lead*

My first week of classes was awesome. Three different middle schools feed into Beauchamp High. So there were new ninth graders I'd never met and who wanted to meet me. I ate in the cafeteria alongside juniors and seniors, mostly from the football team.

Those first few days were more social than academic, with teachers telling you their class rules and giving out books. Except for the bell schedule, it didn't even remind me of middle school. More like having a free pass to an amusement park where one of the biggest attractions had my name and face on it.

Aiden Conroy wasn't my only hater at Beauchamp, though. Maybe half the football team accepted me as the starter, while the other half wanted me to crash and burn.

I guess Cortez didn't belong in either one of those categories. He was a senior defensive tackle—a mountain of a kid with muscles on his muscles, and the team leader on defense. No coach had assigned him that position. He'd earned it over four years and had even played on the Bobcats with Carter two seasons ago.

"What I don't like about freshmen is that they get rattled easy," Cortez told me after cornering me alone at practice. "They play good one game and then disappear the next."

"Not me," I said. "I'm consistent. I—"

Cortez cut me short and said, "Everybody's consistent until they get hit."

Then he shot an arm out to my shoulder and moved me backward two feet.

"Ever been sandwiched by a pair of senior D-linemen?

Each with three years and seventy pounds on your light-weight frame?"

I shook my head.

"I've lifted a lot of weights with your brother. Out of respect for him and the fact that Coach P. picked you, I'm going to support you for now."

"I really appreciate—"

"Don't appreciate anything," he said without taking his arm away. "Just win for us."

During our scrimmage that day, I was wearing the quarterback's bright red practice jersey. It stood out like a stop sign, so every defensive player knew not to hit me. I took a snap and started going through my progression of reads, looking for an open receiver, when Cortez beat a double-team and came motoring at me full-tilt. My whole body tensed, and my fingers locked around the ball an instant before he pulled up—just a few inches away.

"See," he said with his face mask pressed up against mine. "It all looks different when you're about to get hammered."

CHAPTER 14

Some other kids at school seemed to be jealous of what I had. They either snubbed me in the hallway or cut in front of me on the lunch line. I just tried to let it all roll off my back.

Then there was my math teacher, Mrs. Harper, who had a major chip on her shoulder. Five years ago, Carter had her as a freshman. But she'd been at Beauchamp much longer than that. She was almost a senior citizen and completely out of touch, with a weird pointed hairdo that made her look like the grandma of Wolverine from X-Men.

"Travis Gardner, rest assured you won't get any special treatment from me because you've already secured a college scholarship," Mrs. Harper told me as I first passed her desk. "That's the beauty of a mathematics grade. Numbers don't lie. They're not influenced by popularity. Your brother Carter understood his obligations as a student. I hope you have the same work ethic."

That part about my work ethic ticked me off more than anything else.

Besides PE, history had always been my favorite subject. That class looked like it could be a blast. The history teacher, Ms. Orsini, was also my guidance counselor. She was young and fun with a bobbed haircut that swung around her face nearly every time she moved her head.

She'd fooled us all during our first class when she asked, "Where's the Sea of Tranquility?" Kids guessed almost everywhere in the world without getting it right. After we'd run out of places, I even tried, "Inside the Devil's Triangle."

But that was wrong too.

"It's on the Moon. And it's not filled with water. It's a large, dusty crater. It's interesting how we can be deceived by a name."

After class, on my way out the door, Ms. Orsini said, "Travis, I hear you have a lot of big things going on in your life. Drop by the guidance office one day and let's talk about them all. I'd love to hear what's on your mind."

"Sure," I said, thinking there'd be worse ways to spend my time at school.

Lyn Wilson had started at Beauchamp High at the same time as me and her brother, Damon. She wasn't in any of my classes, but we shared the same lunch period.

"Damon told me you're starting quarterback," Lyn said when I saw her in the cafeteria. "That's great."

"Yeah, too bad your bro won't be snapping me the ball," I said.

"I don't think he minds being on the bench. He's not into football the way he used to be," she said. "He's getting interested in bodybuilding."

"I saw all the weight he lost," I said, then changed gears. "Did you go to softball camp this summer?"

"Three weeks. I loved it." She made a windmill motion with her right arm. "Worked a lot on my fastball."

"Hey, I wouldn't want to hit against you."

"That's right. I'd dust you back off the plate."

And I couldn't tell if she was joking with that or warning me not to bother asking her out again.

* * *

At practice, I worked super-hard on my play-fake. Over and over, I'd take the snap, turn around, and put the ball into the running back's stomach. Then, at the last possible moment, I'd pull it out, hiding the ball behind my back. That would slow down a pass rush, making the defense think we'd picked a run play. The safety might even creep up closer to the line, looking to help out on the tackle. Then there'd be less pressure on me and more open receivers. Pisano asked Aiden to show me a few things to polish it up.

"It's all about having a good base," Aiden told me in a condescending voice, putting his two legs into the ground like nothing in the world could move them.

"When you go to pull the ball out, you'd better have your balance. Or else it'll be a disaster."

Aiden worked on that with me for about twenty minutes. When we were done, I tried to give him a pound. Only he left my fist hanging out there. I ran that play-fake during our scrimmage, with Pisano watching on the field from just beyond the D-line.

"Not bad," said Pisano. "Two things a quarterback needs to survive—a good play-fake and a short memory about the mistakes he makes."

Even Cortez, who completely froze in his tracks on a couple of those fakes, gave me a nod of approval. That same day, the team's equipment manager handed out uniforms. I got the number I wanted, the one I'd always worn: twelve. Within five minutes of coming home with my Bobcat jersey, I'd texted a photo of me wearing it to Dad, Carter, and the Gainesville media department, for my Twitter account. I must have looked at myself in the mirror with it on for over an hour, going through different poses with the football and trying to get my expression just right as I imagined my first *Sports Illustrated* cover—somewhere past confident but less obnoxious than cocky.

• • •

Our first game of the season took place on a Friday night in early September, under the lights at Beauchamp. In

Florida, Saturdays are all about college football. They belong to Coach G. and the Gators. But on Fridays, high school football is king. Anytime the Bobcats take the field at home, nearly the entire student body, along with half of Alachua, turns out to watch. We opened up against Santa Fe High. That's the school where Alex played. The Gators were starting their season the next night at home. So Carter and Alex had come with Mom to see me play. I ran up to them near the stands, about an hour before game time.

"Are you rooting for Travis tonight or your old school?" Carter asked Alex in front of me.

"Sorry, lil bro," Alex said, shaking his head. "I hope you throw five touchdown passes and make all the newspapers. But I want to see my Raiders score six TDs."

"I thought we were *fam*," I teased Alex.

"We are. But on the field, football trumps family. That's how blood brothers can whip each other's butts and still go home to the same dinner table. It's *off* the field that fam wins out."

"Sounds smart," Mom said, looking at me and Carter. "At home, it should always be family first, not competition."

I blew Mom a kiss and started backpedaling toward the field, not wanting to hear a longer lecture from her.

Then I pointed at Alex and said, "I'm going to kick Santa Fe tail tonight. You'll just have to smile and suck it up."

All through the warm-ups, my nerves were tighter than I'd let on to anyone. I heard one of our players say he thought he'd seen Coach G. in the stands. I didn't believe it for a second, not with the Gators playing a game in twenty-four hours. Still, it gave me goose bumps.

We won the coin toss, and Pisano wanted the football first.

After the thump of the ball coming off the Santa Fe kicker's shoe, our special teams returned the kickoff to our own thirty-six-yard line. I put on my helmet, tightened the chinstrap, and listened to the applause as I jogged onto the field.

On our first play from scrimmage, I stepped to the line and looked over the Santa Fe defense. Their coach must have been convinced Pisano would take the pressure off me and begin by running the ball. He was right. Santa Fe had eight of their eleven defenders crowding the line, ready to stop our runner cold. So I decided to call an audible and change the play at the line.

"Omaha! Omaha!" I hollered out left and then right. "Eighteen rocket! Eighteen rocket! Hut!"

My voice was still echoing inside the stadium as the center snapped the ball. I took a quick two-step drop and spotted our slot receiver slanting across the middle. I planted my right foot into the ground. Then, my left arm, up around the ear hole of my helmet, whipped forward with the football. I could visualize a bull's-eye on my receiver's chest—and I fired the pass right on target.

The cheers were almost deafening as our receiver streaked downfield for a forty-yard gain. They became the soundtrack to confidence building inside of me, beating back every last doubt.

There were more than fifty plays on a five-inch-long wristband attached to my right forearm. Pisano would send in the call. Then I'd find its number on the band and give the play to our offense.

I broke the huddle with a loud clap of my hands. Ten other guys on offense were moving in rhythm to *me*. I handed the ball off to our fullback, who gained a few yards. But I stayed extremely conscious of the position of my legs, waist, and shoulders. A couple of plays later, using that exact same form, I turned to hand the ball off again. Only, this time, I pulled the ball out from our fullback's stomach. It was a perfect play-fake, and Raider defense took the bait, with the safety cheating up. Standing calmly in the pocket, I rifled the ball downfield. It spiraled through the air without wavering an inch. My receiver hauled it in and raced into the end zone.

We took a 7-to-0 lead, but that was just the start.

I stood on the sideline with my helmet off, gazing into the stands. I was trying not to smile too wide or too often, wanting people to believe this was nothing out of the ordinary for me. I was talking to *all* of my teammates, and they were *all* talking back.

After that, I connected on my next nine passes. I was dropping balls into every open window, no matter how small. The Santa Fe D couldn't do a thing to stop it.

Just being out there gave me the most incredible feeling, the reason I started playing quarterback to begin with. The same feeling had hit me when I was a little kid, tossing the ball around with Dad and Carter. But now I was sharing it with an entire stadium full of fans. I wanted to keep that feeling forever. I wanted to ride it through four years of high school, and maybe win a state championship, before cruising into Gainesville to quarterback the Gators.

We crushed Santa Fe, 37–6.

I prayed Coach G. would catch the highlights on the local sports report and that ESPN would give me a shout-out. Now I had a win to back up all the hype. My teammates were looking at me like I was their leader. And I'd erased any last doubts about who should be the Bobcats' quarterback.

CHAPTER 15

The next day, Saturday, I arrived at Carter and Alex's dorm room before noon. I couldn't get enough football. I put off any homework I had just to be there early and hang around. The Gators were opening their season against Appalachian State that night. It was supposed to be a real cupcake game, with Gainesville favored by nearly four touchdowns.

Alex was finishing a set of five hundred sit-ups, twisting his midsection to touch his elbows to the opposite knee and letting out an *umph* with each one.

Carter sat at his desk, going back and forth between his playbook and a chapter in some reading for a political science class. I settled on the floor with my back up against Carter's bed, playing *Angry Birds* on my brother's laptop.

"This game's addictive," I said, using a slingshot to launch another bird at those stupid pigs.

Alex popped up off the floor and asked me to mute the volume.

"I'm going to grab some shut-eye," Alex said, stretching out on the other bed in the room. "Team meal's at three-thirty. Wake me up fifteen minutes before that."

Then he buried his face beneath a pillow. The game wasn't the same without the sound. So I started searching around the room for something else to do.

"Help me study," Carter said in a quiet voice. "You can quiz me on my notes."

"I don't know anything about political science," I told him. "I'm not even old enough to vote."

"I was talking about my playbook," Carter said.

"Really? You told me that was super-secret stuff. For Gators' eyes only," I said.

"You're a season closer now. But hey, if you don't want to help . . ."

"No, I'll do it," I said, taking the notes from his hand.

For nearly an hour, we went through all the play calls, audibles, and check-downs at the line of scrimmage. Carter had them pretty much memorized, but I helped him on a few. At the very end, I started calling out audibles for him like I was changing the play at the line myself.

Out of nowhere, Carter grinned wide and said, "Breakdown on the O-line." Then he pounced from his chair and tackled me to the floor. "Quarterback sack!"

That's when Alex jumped out of his bed, hollering, "What's with you clowns? I asked for quiet, right? Can't sleep for nothing around here!"

He stormed into the bathroom, slamming the door shut behind him.

CARTER'S TAKE

PEDs—that was the only way I could explain what I'd witnessed. But there was no way I could tell that to Travis, who seemed completely shook.

Four or five times over the last few weeks, Alex had blown up over nothing. But this was more intense than any of the others—an absolute explosion.

"Think we should apologize for the noise?" Travis asked me.

"No, it's probably best to let it go for now. He's always uptight before a game and cranky when he wakes up," I answered, staring at the closed bathroom door. "Why don't you go down to the complex for a while? Let me talk to Alex alone. You know, roommate stuff."

"All right. I'll look for Harkey," Travis said, moving toward the door to the hall. "He wanted to talk to me anyway, about starting on some kind of supplement."

"You know what?" I said, hooking him around the shoulder. "Harkey's always real busy on game days. Let's talk to him about supplements some other time, *together.* Why don't you see if the equipment manager needs help setting out the helmets. And don't spit inside mine."

"Hey, thanks for the idea, bro," Travis said, regaining a smile.

After Travis left, I stood right outside the bathroom. I was worried that Alex could be doping at that moment. Then I came to my senses. I realized that no matter what, the Alex I knew would never do anything like that with my brother hanging around. Unless those PEDs had totally changed his thinking.

I couldn't just stand there forever, hoping to figure it out.

"You okay?" I asked, gently knocking at the door.

"No sleep *and* no privacy, huh?" Alex replied.

From inside, I heard the squeak of a faucet being turned and the shower starting to run.

Alex could make his own decisions. His body. His choice. If he was hurting anyone, it was himself.

But as I hit the hallway to go after Travis, the questions I'd been dodging began echoing in my mind louder than ever: Who's supplying Alex, and how's he paying for it?

CHAPTER 16

The Gators' game against Appalachian State didn't go as planned. The Mountaineers held a 10-to-9 lead at half-time. I'd stood on the sideline for a while behind Coach Goddard. He got angrier and angrier over every mistake his team made. And by the end of the first half, he was breathing fire.

"You know why they call it an *upset?*" raged Coach G. in the locker room, with the whole team gathered around him. "Because some glue-factory nag named *Upset* beat Man o' War, the greatest racehorse of all time. That's what these guys are, compared to you— *mules.* They couldn't get scholarships to a real football school. They didn't have the talent. But they're beating *you.* They want to steal your dreams of a national title. You're supposed to be the thoroughbreds here. Perform like it!"

He slammed a marker against a dry-erase board and walked off. The assistant coaches for defense, special teams, and receivers pulled their players together in small groups to start making adjustments. Alex had caught five first-half passes. He'd been the whole offense and the main reason the Gators were trailing by a single point, not more.

Right before the Gators left the locker room, Alex spoke to the team.

"Hear me, my brothers. This game of football's my life. It's where I'm going. It's who I am. I know for lots of you it's the same," Alex said, holding his helmet in one hand and his mouthpiece in the other. "There's no second-best in me. The true talent's on *our* sideline, not theirs. I'm going to push twice as hard to get this done. Not for tonight, but for this entire season. I'll prove that to you all, every practice, every game. All I want to know is, who's with me?"

Carter was the first one to shout, "Gators!"

Then a hundred other voices, including mine, shouted it too.

I was ready to put my head down and run through a brick wall after hearing Alex's speech. And I didn't even have a helmet.

* * *

Appalachian State didn't disappear in the second half. They kept fighting hard and making plays. But the Gators' size and strength started to wear the Mountaineers down in the fourth quarter.

Late in the game, Carter leaped up, trying to snag a pass for a big first down and keep a drive alive. I never saw him get up so high, not even off a diving board in the Alachua Community Pool. At the height of his leap, a defender hit him in the thigh, sending Carter into a mid-air backflip. He crashed to the ground, clamping his fingers around the ball a split-second before it touched the turf.

I clapped so hard for Carter that my palms stung.

On the next play from scrimmage, Alex caught a short pass and made a Mountaineer miss a tackle. He burst into the open, dodging defenders like a deer cutting in and out of trees. That long gain by Alex set up the game-winning field goal. The Gators survived, 22–20. In the locker room, Coach G. gave Alex the game ball.

"Remember what I pledged," Alex told the team, taking the ball from Goddard's hands. "All out. Twice as hard, every day. I won't let you down. Just be sure that none of you let yourselves down."

* * *

That night and most of the next day, Alex's speech was on my mind. I wanted to be that kind of leader and work as hard as he did. Then, on Sunday night, with a couple of unfinished homework assignments spread out across my bed, I got down on the floor for a set of five hundred sit-ups.

I could hear Alex's speech ringing in my ears—
football's my life . . . no second-best in me . . . it's who I am.
The echo of his voice pushed me past the pain. It helped
me outlast the tightening knots in my stomach muscles,
all the way to five hundred.

Those final ten sit-ups felt amazing. Despite the
strain, knowing I was going to make it brought me
nothing but joy.

"Four ninety-seven. Four ninety-eight. Four ninety-
nine. Five hundred."

I was sweating so much, I needed to change my
shirt and towel off or I'd drip sweat all over my assignments. The endorphins pumping through my body
had me feeling too good for homework. Instead, I
phoned Damon, just to talk about football for a few
minutes.

"You played great on Friday. I know. I watched
almost every down from our bench," said Damon, who
only got into the game on a few plays. "But there's a
question I've wanted to ask for a while."

"Go ahead," I said.

"Is football still fun for you? I mean the way it used
to be, like when we were kids playing in the park?"

It took me a couple of seconds to get my mind in
gear before I could answer his question.

"Yeah, I'm having fun. Who wouldn't? Why would
you even ask me something like that?"

"Ever since they gave you the scholarship," Damon

said, "it looks more like work. Like football's your *job* now."

I didn't know what to say, but the buzz from those endorphins began to wear off.

"Well, it's not exactly easy. I've got something to live up to on every snap, every game. But it's nothing I didn't ask for. That's the challenge of being quarterback. It's all in my hands," I said, and then changed the subject to how Damon was dealing with his role on the Bobcats.

I could barely listen to him, though, filling up my end with an "I hear you" every now and then. Damon's question wouldn't leave me alone. When the conversation was over, I felt a little numb. The sensation started in the tips of my fingers, working its way down my arms to my core. But I convinced myself it was all because of the sit-ups.

⚜ ⚜ ⚜

Monday morning at school, my name seemed to have replaced the regular hallway chatter. I couldn't turn my head around without hearing praise about the game I'd played Friday night.

My haters, however many of them were left, kept their mouths shut.

Walking between classes was like stepping through some incredible dream, until a guy on the Bobcats came up from behind me with his iPhone out.

"Travis, you hear the news yet?" he asked.

"No, what news?"

"One of the Gators died at football practice this morning," he said, showing me the *Sentinel* website.

"What? How?" I asked, with my blood turning cold. The image of Carter's face filled my mind. "Who? Who was it?"

As I searched the text beneath the headline for a name, my teammate said, "Their receiver, the guy from Santa Fe High. Alex Moore."

My insides started shaking and wouldn't stop. I couldn't tell if I was about to puke or cry.

THE GAINESVILLE SENTINEL

Section D/Sports – Columnists

FIGHTIN' GATOR ALEX MOORE DIES OF HEART FAILURE

KAREN WOLFENDALE

Alex Moore, a junior wide receiver for the Gainesville University football program, collapsed due to an apparent heart failure during drills at practice yesterday morning. Emergency medical technicians rushed Moore to North Florida Medical Center, where he was pronounced dead on arrival at 9:32 EST.

Team doctors gave Moore a clean bill of health at the start of the season, following surgery to repair a torn ACL in his left knee earlier this year. This past Saturday, the receiver recorded eleven receptions and was instrumental in a hard-fought Gator victory, finishing the game without any apparent health issues.

"It's a stunning blow for our program and the university," said Head Coach Elvis Goddard. "Alex Moore was an inspiration to everyone on this team. He was totally committed to fight back from his injury and to play to the very best of his God-given abilities. The only solace we have is that Alex spent his last minutes on this earth surrounded by his teammates—his football family, preparing for the game he loved. I'm sure that his spirit and memory will remain a vital part of this team."

ESPN football analysts had projected Moore as a late first-round or early second-round pick in next year's NFL draft. Moore had no history of heart disease. He is survived by his mother, Dorothy Moore, of Alachua.

According to published studies, approximately one out of every 200,000 athletes dies due to unexpected cardiac arrest each year. The event is usually precipitated by physical activity.

"Alex was the hardest worker I ever knew," said Carter Gardner, who was Moore's roommate and the first to reach him on the practice field after he collapsed. "Alex was holding on with everything he had. I could see it in his eyes. He fought until his heart stopped beating. After the EMTs put Alex in the ambulance, we all held hands in a circle and got down on one knee to pray."

Funeral services for Alex Moore are scheduled for Friday at 10:00 a.m. at Calvary Baptist Church in Alachua.

The Gators play their next game the following night at home against Furman University.

CHAPTER 17

The only funerals I'd been to before were for old people, like my two grandpas. But they'd both been sick for a long time first. This was different. Alex was an athlete. He was young and strong. Even though he wasn't part of my *real* family, his death hit me ten times as hard.

Alex's wake was held on Thursday afternoon and through the evening. Mom made me go to school on Thursday, because I was already going to miss classes Friday for the funeral. I went to Thursday practice too, preparing for our game the next night. I raced back home to take a five-minute shower. Then I wolfed down some leftover ravioli before jumping into the car with Mom. She got lost on the drive over to the funeral home. Part of me hoped we'd never get there. But eventually we did.

"Hold still," Mom said, retying my tie for the second time, after we finally found a parking space. "Walter Henry's knots always look perfect. Maybe you could ask him to show you how he does it."

"Remember when I could wear those clip-on ties?"

"Those were the easy days. You're too grown-up for those now," she said, getting out of the car and smoothing out her skirt.

My legs shook as we walked through the front door of the funeral home. The place was packed with people. And in every direction I looked, somebody was crying.

Coach G. and Harkey were standing outside the viewing room, having what looked like a private conversation in the corner. So I didn't try to get their attention as Mom walked me past. Once we got inside, I saw Carter. He'd been there all day with his teammates, and his eyes were completely red.

"I'm glad you're here, Trav," he said, putting an arm around my shoulder and pulling me in close. "I've been thinking about you a lot today."

"About *me*?" I asked. "Why?"

"Because you're a great brother," he answered, squeezing me a little harder.

I couldn't remember the last time Carter said something like that.

"I just can't believe I'll never see Alex flying down a football field again," I said. "I'll never forget that day he beat Galaxy in a race."

Carter nodded his head and started to choke up. That's when he turned me loose, and walked off to be alone.

Walter Henry had come to the wake too, sitting alone at the back of the room. He didn't look anything like himself. His swagger was nonexistent. He wore dark glasses and was using a handkerchief to smother the tears running down his cheeks. I don't think he even noticed me that night. I knew Walter and Alex were close. I had figured Walter would become Alex's agent when he made it to the NFL. And now he looked completely broken up.

"You ready to go up to the casket and pay your respects?" Mom asked me.

"Another minute or two," I answered, not wanting to come face to face with Alex's body.

"You know, you don't have to," Mom said. "We're really here for Alex's mother. Maybe we should go see her first."

"All right," I said.

She was sitting in the first row of chairs, wearing a black veil that came down just over her eyes.

"Bless you for being here, child," she said to me.

"We're so sorry for your loss," Mom said, in almost a whisper.

I just nodded, not knowing what else to add.

"Your oldest son was a good friend to my boy. I want you to know I appreciate that," she said, grasping Mom's hand and then mine.

A digital photo frame sat on a small table a couple of feet from the casket. Every few seconds, it flashed to another image from Alex's life. There was a photo of Alex making a catch in his Gator uniform, one of him celebrating in the end zone, one of him graduating high school, and one of Alex with his mother behind the counter at the sub shop. Then a photo came on the screen from when Alex was much younger, maybe a few years younger than me. He stood next to a tall, lanky man with an athletic build. The two were smiling, and each had a hand on the football between them.

"That was Alex's father," said Carter, coming up from behind me. "His mother told me they were really close. That's maybe why he didn't talk about his father much—it made Alex so sad to lose him."

That's when I pulled up all the courage I had and walked over to the casket. Inside, Alex was lying there like he was asleep. He'd been dressed in a dark blue suit. Over that, he wore his blue Gator home jersey, number eighty-eight. On his cheek, there was a small smear of red lipstick, the same shade his mother was wearing. My eyes followed the outline of the two eights on his jersey, tracing each one until they crossed back along the same path.

"Double-infinity," I said to myself. "Take care, bro. Wherever you are, I hope you're with your dad."

As I stood back up, Carter came over to take my place in front of Alex.

CARTER'S TAKE

Don't worry, fam. I won't let you down this time. Not like I did before. It was the biggest mistake of my life—the day you told me you were on PEDs and I didn't do a thing to stop it. I figured that you could make your own decisions. I talked myself into that, to justify it. But I was completely blind. I didn't see how much pressure you were putting on yourself, trying to recover from that blown-out knee.

Now everybody believes you're a hero. They say that you worked yourself to death trying to make this team better, trying to make us all better. Well, that's the way it's going to stay. I promise. I owe you that. I thought about telling somebody what I know. But I couldn't break that kind of news to your mother. Not after seeing how proud she is. I even thought about telling Coach. But if you really did get those drugs from somebody connected to the program, the NCAA might rip this whole team apart from top to bottom. I know that's something you would have never wanted.

Right now, the doctors say it was strictly your heart— that there was nothing else in your system. I know better. We both do. But that's where it's going to stay, between you and me and whoever sold you that poison. If that dude was in front of me, I'd beat him into the ground, I swear. But don't worry. I got your back. No one's ever going to lose respect for you. No one's ever going to call you a cheater. Your mother's never going to feel that shame. Your name's never going to take that hit. God bless you, fam.

CHAPTER 18

At the cemetery the next day, after the preacher spoke, I stood in a long line of mourners. We were all waiting to toss a handful of dirt into Alex's grave. Some people dropped their dirt in all at once. Others did it a little bit at a time. When it was my turn, I grabbed the dirt from a huge pile, then stood over the grave with my eyes closed and let it slowly slip through my fingers. Just before we were ready to leave, a work crew of three men holding shovels showed up, getting ready to fill the rest of the hole where Alex was buried.

Carter left with his teammates, and I drove back with Mom. It was almost noon, and I wanted Mom to take me home instead of school. That's when Coach Pisano called my phone.

"Travis, whatever you do, get back here before the end of the day," Pisano said.

"Why, Coach? What's wrong?' I asked.

"It's your math teacher, the lovely Mrs. Harper," said Pisano. "I've been through this with her before.

You're not supposed to play in the game tonight if you're absent, and Harper's a stickler. As soon as you missed her class this morning, she sent a note to me *and* Principal Ross."

"All right, I'm coming there now." I pressed End and then turned to Mom, saying something she probably never dreamed would come out of my mouth: "Hurry up. Get me to school as fast as you can."

I got there for sixth period, still wearing my suit. I didn't even have a notebook with me, so I borrowed a pen and paper, prepared to sit through the rest of the school day. Eighth period was my final stop: PE with Coach Pisano. He told me to sit on the side and study up on our game plan rather than change into my gym clothes.

"There's going to be a meeting about this Harper nonsense in the principal's office right after class. I want you dressed just the way you are now. Don't even loosen your tie," Pisano said.

When Coach and I got to the office, Mrs. Harper was already there. She stopped talking to the principal the second I walked in. Ms. Orsini, my history teacher and guidance counselor, came through the door after I did.

"Travis, I was just on the phone with your mother. How are you coping?" Ms. Orsini asked. "Funerals are never easy. They can make us feel very uncertain about lots of things."

"I'm hanging in," I answered, realizing that she was

the only teacher so far to ask me something like that.

"Is that where you were this morning, Travis? At a funeral?" Principal Ross asked.

"Yes, sir. For Alex Moore, the Gator who died. He was my brother's roommate. I trained with him all summer on the Gainesville campus," I said, feeling the sadness well up inside me.

Ms. Orsini took a tissue off the principal's desk and tried to hand it to me. But I wouldn't take it, not in front of Coach P.

"His lateness seems legitimate," Principal Ross told Mrs. Harper. "I don't see a reason he should be made ineligible for the game."

"I disagree," said Mrs. Harper. "This isn't about a funeral. It's about Mr. Gardner acting like a scholarship athlete instead of a high school student. It's another excuse for football over academics."

"Is she kidding?" Pisano asked the principal.

"This wasn't even a relative of Mr. Gardner," Mrs. Harper said.

That's when I couldn't hold back anymore.

"Alex *was* family to me!" I snapped, with tears starting to stream down my face. "Maybe you don't care about yours, but I do!"

The room paused around me as I struggled to catch my breath.

"You can wait outside now, Travis," Principal Ross said in a soft tone.

Ms. Orsini came with me, bringing more tissues.

I pulled myself together as fast as I could.

"Sometimes it's better to let it all out," she said to me in the principal's outer office.

"Not for a varsity quarterback, it isn't," I said, wiping the last of the tears from my eyes.

Pisano walked out next and said, "You're playing tonight. Just make up the work you missed in math today." Then he turned to Ms. Orsini.

"I appreciate your help in there," Pisano told her as he pulled me into the hall.

"I wasn't helping you *or* the football team," I heard Ms. Orsini say from over my shoulder. "I was there for Travis."

◆ ◆ ◆

When I walked into our locker room before the game, I noticed Aiden Conroy's name and uniform number had disappeared from over his locker.

"Talk is he transferred to Citrus High. To try and be the starting quarterback there," Damon told me. "Guess you crushed all his hopes with that big game you had last week."

"Too bad," I said, trying to downplay it. "That's one less good athlete on our team. Hurts our depth."

But on the inside, a surge of satisfaction ran through me.

Other players weren't being so nice, especially Cortez.

"He's a traitor and a punk," Cortez said, lacing up his cleats. "He put himself ahead of this team and his school."

Most of our guys on defense were already planning to pay Aiden back with pain when we played Citrus in a few weeks.

I stopped into Pisano's office to talk about it.

"Conroy has an aunt who lives in that school district. His parents signed a notarized letter claiming he's moved in with her," said Pisano. "*Our* problem is that he knows our entire offense. He'll tell their coaching staff everything. We'll have to make changes when we play them."

"Not a problem. I can handle it."

"Good. I wanted to speak to you before the game anyway," Pisano said. "You've shown plenty of poise for a freshman so far. But coming off that funeral, I want to make sure you have a handle on your emotions tonight. Don't get too high or too low. Concentrate on your fundamentals."

"Calmness and execution," I said. "That's what Coach G. told me about quarterbacking the first day I met him."

"I like that," Pisano said. "You know, he's the reason I gave you the starting job."

"Because he saw something special in me?" I asked.

"I suppose that's part of it, sure. For a freshman you're terrific, very advanced. Travis, I'm hoping to develop you over four years here. That's about the time I'm looking to retire from the high school ranks. I wouldn't mind being rewarded by Elvis Goddard with an assistant coaching job on the Gators' staff. Sort of a thank-you for delivering his top prospect right on schedule."

I nodded my head, and left his office feeling a little bit like a piece of meat.

CHAPTER 19

Four hours after my talk with Coach Pisano, I was gearing up for our game against Eastside High. I pushed Alex's death behind some dark curtain inside my head and concentrated on football. That had always been one of the best parts about being on the field: there weren't any outside problems. Right then, only the game mattered. Everything else just vanished. It was like I didn't have parents who were divorced, an older brother to compete with, or headaches over grades at school. For sixty minutes of game clock, I didn't have a single worry in the world, not as long as I was playing quarterback.

Before I took the field, Cortez came up to me.

"Hey, you showed up big last week. But it was all Bobcats from start to finish. Nobody rocked you," he said. "New game tonight. If things begin to go wrong, make sure you don't pull that disappearing act I warned you about. Don't become an empty uniform out there."

"I'm solid," I said, tapping my chest. "And I'm hungry for another win."

"You'd better be. That Eastside D is thinking *freshman* means fresh meat."

On my first series of the game, I had a Bobcat receiver ready to run a deep route down the far sideline. The Eastside defense was covering us man to man. At the snap of the ball, I looked to the other side of the field, freezing the safety in the middle and stopping him from sliding over to help out. Then I turned back to my receiver running that deep route.

His defender ran with him stride for stride, covering him like a blanket.

My receiver had a few inches on the guy. So I had thoughts of throwing it up for grabs and giving my guy a chance to win a jump ball. But as the football was about to leave my hand, I saw my receiver's eyes start to turn toward me.

Within a fraction of a second, I read the move. That's when I purposely threw the ball toward his back shoulder instead of leading him down the field. Two strides later, my receiver slowed up just enough to let his defender run past. Then he reached back for the football, snagging it for a long gain.

A few snaps after that, we had a broken play. Two of our receivers nearly collided when one of them ran the wrong route. I scrambled, looking for somewhere to go. As I prepared to throw the ball away, out of bounds, I recognized the body language of our tight end. He gave his defender this little shifting move, something I'd seen him do at practice a bunch of times. So I had the ball heading to him before he made his cut to be wide open in the end zone.

It was like my receivers and I were thinking with the same brain. Totally in sync.

I even took my first sack on our following offensive series. A heavyweight Eastside lineman beat our O-line clean off the snap. He came lumbering at me in our backfield. I lost my footing and got stuck in his sights. I ducked down, like I was trying to dive beneath a monster wave at the beach. He pounded me pretty hard. But I went with his momentum and didn't try to fight his force. I bounced up off the ground right away.

That called for eye contact with Cortez on our sideline. I gave him a nod to show I could take a *real* hit. The guys in my huddle had their eyes on me too. I took the play Pisano sent in and found it on my wristband. Then I called it out for them, loud and strong, before I stood tall in the pocket and completed my next pass.

Everything was going great. We had a thirteen-point lead. Cortez even sacked the Eastside QB, glancing over at me afterward to return the nod.

Then, early in the third quarter, it happened.

I was on the sideline, sipping from a cup of Gatorade.

The Eastside quarterback threw a high spiral down the middle. His receiver cut across the field, leaping up to catch it. One of our D-backs absolutely drilled him, burying his shoulder pads into the receiver's chest and causing the loudest pop I'd heard in a long time. I could almost feel the hit from where I was standing. I thought that receiver might not get back up. Eastside's trainer probably figured the same, because he was already running onto the field toward the guy.

But that receiver jumped to his feet, shaking off the hit like it was nothing.

That's when I saw he was wearing number eighty-eight, Alex's double-infinity.

The receiver spun the ball onto the ground with one hand before pounding a fist to his chest. I swear, he was looking straight at me as he shouted, "Nothing in this world can break me! Nothing!"

A wicked chill ran through my body.

All my inner defenses disappeared. That dark curtain I hid things behind was torn to shreds. I couldn't keep the thought of Alex's death from creeping into my mind. And I couldn't watch Eastside on offense for another play, all because I didn't want to catch sight of that receiver again.

Back on the field, my concentration started to slip away. No matter how hard I tried to hold my emotions back, I could feel the flood taking me over.

I got sacked again. Only this time, I rose up feeling battered and numb.

My accuracy suffered for the rest of the game, with passes drifting off-target.

I had a tough time finding the plays on my wristband too. The distraction even caused a pair of delay-of-game penalties.

"Keep your head in the game, Gardner," Pisano barked. "Everything's in front of you, not off to the sides."

Somehow, though, I managed to hold myself together through the fourth quarter, completing a couple of passes, and we beat Eastside 23 to 18.

Walking off the field, Cortez looked me up and down. "You got rattled, but you're still here. That's more than I can say about our former QB."

@TravisG_Gator *Bobcats win, 2-0. As a starting QB, after the final whistle, I threw 1 more pass deep dwn field for Alex Moore, RIP Fam!*

While the Gators were dressing for their game on Saturday, one of Alex's jerseys hung inside his open locker. Players passed by it and crossed themselves or bowed their heads, like it was a sort of shrine. They'd drawn 88 on their cleats with Sharpies too. I reached inside the locker and ran my fingers over the fabric, trying to feel Alex's spirit.

"Dad call you this week?" Carter asked me, from his locker next to Alex's.

"Yeah, late last night."

"Talk about anything special?"

"My game, a lot about Alex's funeral and stuff," I answered.

"What he say?"

"What you'd expect. That dying is part of life. Accept it and move on."

"Know what he told *me*?" Carter said. "I should tell the dean of students that my roommate dying is going to make it impossible for me to keep my mind on studying. He thinks the school would probably give me straight As this semester because of it."

"Really? I never heard of anything like that."

"I told him I didn't want a free ride on Alex's death. That I didn't deserve it."

"What'd Dad say?" I asked.

"That I shouldn't take things so personally."

"Like when he threatened to take Mom to court, to lower our child support payments?"

"*I still love you boys. It's just the way the system works,*" said Carter, with a near-perfect imitation of Dad's voice.

I stared back at Alex's jersey and asked, "Ever feel like we've been halfway cheated out of having a dad? I mean, with the divorce and him moving to California?"

"I feel just like you do, Trav," Carter answered, putting on his pads. "Just hope neither one of us ever feels like we were halfway cheated out of having a brother."

A moment later, Coach Goddard stepped out of his office. He took Alex's jersey from the locker and handed it to me.

"I want this on our sideline tonight for inspiration," Goddard said. "Travis, it's your job to make sure it never touches the ground."

I nodded my head, going back and forth between his eyes and Carter's.

"Big responsibility," Carter said to me.

"I've got it," I said, with the jersey already feeling a few ounces heavier.

Right before the Gators left their locker room, Coach G. gave his pre-game speech.

"I don't know what's waiting for us on the other side of life," he said, laying a hand to the front of Alex's jersey. His voice filled more of the room with each word. "Maybe the answer to that is different for every one of us. I can only tell you this much for sure. If Alex had one more opportunity to put on this uniform and play football for the Gators, he'd devour it. *You* have that opportunity, each one of you. Appreciate it. Be thankful. Don't squander it. Alex's mother will be in the stands. Play for her. Play for Alex's memory. Play for the family that surrounds you right now—this team."

Carter rushed his hand forward to touch Alex's jersey. A frenzy of other arms reached out for it after that.

Harkey shouted, "Everybody, on three! *One team! One family!* . . . One, two, three—"

"One team! One family!" we shouted together.

The Gators steamrolled Furman that night, taking a 28–0 lead after the first quarter. But as the game wore on, Alex's jersey got heavier and heavier to hold.

Carter caught six passes. He hauled one in at the five-yard line before dragging three Furman defenders on his back into the end zone. Rather than spiking the ball, though, Carter walked it over to the first row of the stands and gave it to Alex's mother.

By the fourth quarter, my arms were aching. Even my legs felt the strain. Twice, the jersey almost slipped out of my hands and touched the ground. But I was able to steady myself both times. With less than a minute to go in the game, Carter took the jersey from me. He held it high over his head for the crowd to see. A thunderstorm of applause came in return. Only, I was too exhausted to even clap.

* * *

That next week at practice, I had my mind fixed on football. I was completely zoned in, refusing to let anything else wreck my concentration. After my miserable second half against Eastside, I had dropped out of the ten top-ranked passers in the state. But I was still undefeated as a high school quarterback and I had picked up a ton more Twitter followers.

Beauchamp's student store started selling black-and-gold jerseys with GARDNER printed across the back. I was hyped to see kids wearing them around school. I even autographed a few.

While I was signing one for a girl in the cafeteria, I noticed Lyn had spotted me.

"You really enjoy that?" Lyn asked afterward, once I'd parked myself next to her with my tray.

"Just giving my fans what they want, being a gentleman," I answered, shaking my container of chocolate milk. "I *am* the varsity quarterback."

"You don't have to remind me," said Lyn. "Did you know Damon's thinking about quitting the football team?"

"That's crazy. We could be state champs. Is it because he's not getting enough playing time?"

"No. He wants to train for some bodybuilding competitions. He's getting pretty serious about being in shape."

"I need to talk to him more, find out what he's thinking," I told her. "I've been too distracted lately. I'll take care of it."

Then I finally got down to the reason I'd sat next to Lyn.

"So you want to get together soon? Catch a movie?" I asked.

"You're so busy being a *gentleman*, I'm surprised you'd have the time. Anyway, I have a full schedule coming up—school and social."

"Whatever," I said, absorbing that minor hit.

Anyway, I figured I wouldn't have to look too hard to find another female fan.

＊ ＊ ＊

Later that week, in Mrs. Harper's math class, we were doing conversion charts. One question from the book read like someone had written it especially for me: *An NFL quarterback throws a football 60 yards. How many feet does the football travel?*

I raised my hand up high. It was the most excited I'd ever been in her class, with the answer sitting on the tip of my tongue. But Mrs. Harper didn't pick me, probably on purpose. Instead, she chose some girl who got it wrong.

A few minutes later, she passed me up again. I was really annoyed. She must have seen on my face how bad I wanted to be called on.

As the next kid gave the right answer, I said, in a voice just beneath his, "One hundred and eighty feet."

I sulked in my seat for the rest of the period. On the way out, I walked past Mrs. Harper's desk as slow as I could, almost staring her down.

"I understood that you knew the answer, Travis. I'd have been greatly disappointed if you didn't," Mrs. Harper said. "I'm more interested in seeing you learn something *new* this semester."

"It'd be nice to get some credit for what I already know," I said, leaving without softening the look on my face.

CHAPTER 20

I sent Dad one of the Beauchamp High jerseys with my name on it. Only, his reaction wasn't anything like I thought it would be.

"I think we need to be careful with your name," Dad said. "I've researched it a bit. Amateur athletes can't make money endorsing products. But that doesn't mean we can't begin to shape your public image. Then when you're finished playing in college, corporations will be lining up for you to represent them."

"Do we really have to worry about this now?" I asked.

"Travis, the average NFL playing career is just over three years. And that's if you make it."

"*If?*" I said. "I don't know any other high school freshman with jersey sales."

"There are no guarantees in life. That's why you take advantage of these opportunities and market yourself while you're hot."

"Last time I checked, Coach G. *did* give me a guarantee. At least to make the team and be a Gator."

"It doesn't bind him to anything, Travis. Remember that. So we've got to be smart."

I didn't expect my quarterbacking skills to cool off anytime soon. So after that, I just answered, "Sure. Sure," to all of Dad's concerns.

* * *

The next game on the Beauchamp schedule put us on the road, against Chiles, one of the weakest teams in our division. On paper, their defense looked like Swiss cheese. I was drooling at the idea of going up against them, to really pad my passing stats.

Lots of kids from Beauchamp made the bus trip to see us play, and there were plenty of Gardner jerseys in the stands. In the visitors' locker room, I drew *#88* on my cleats, like Carter and his teammates had. This way, I'd be carrying part of Alex's memory with me, instead of fighting myself to block it out. Before kickoff, I went to find Cortez.

"I'm going to give sixty minutes today. Count on it," I told him. "I figure my offense is good for at least forty points. All your D has to do is hold them to less than that."

Cortez grinned so wide, the dark hairs over his upper lip spread apart.

"That's what I like, a quarterback with confidence," he said. "I hope you're talking that way two weeks from now, when we play Lincoln. I want to see your face after you get a look at those monsters."

"I'm not scared of *any* defense," I said, spinning a ball in my left hand. "They should all be scared of me."

"Hang on tight to that ego. You're going to need it," Cortez said, spreading his helmet at the earflaps to fit it over his head. "Just make sure it doesn't get too big for you to carry."

* * *

The Chiles defense played five or six yards off every one of our receivers. That extra cushion was like buttercream frosting on a red velvet cake with my name on it.

I put every ball I threw right on the numbers. Even if those defenders had been glued to my receivers at the hip, it wouldn't have mattered. I was so hot, I would have delivered the football into any window, no matter how small.

Every time Pisano sent in a running play, I groaned. I called an audible on a few of them, changing the plays to passes. All I wanted to do was throw the football against a defense that didn't want to step up.

I'd connected on my first twelve passes when the equipment manager told me the Beauchamp High record for consecutive completions stood at thirteen. We were already ahead 21–0. So I focused on getting my name into the record book.

"Soon as we get the ball back, I want to try that deep crossing route we've been working on in practice," Pisano told me on the sideline, while our defense was on the field. "Let's work on the timing in a game situation, so we have it down on a day we really need it."

The deep cross involved a risky pass and a route our receivers hadn't run a lot. But I couldn't tell Pisano I wanted that record without sounding selfish.

When the time came for Chiles to punt the ball back to us, I peeked at my wristband for a more high-percentage pass. I called Pisano's play in the huddle—but I already knew I was going to audible out of it.

At the line of scrimmage, I looked over the Chiles defense. Their D was still giving our receivers plenty of cushion, playing back on its heels. A short pass would be almost an automatic completion.

"Tango! Tango!" I barked, letting my offense know I was changing the play call. "Sightline! Sightline!"

I followed that with some numbers and code words that had no meaning. My receivers knew *sightline* meant the ball was coming to one of them right away.

I took the snap and immediately pivoted to my left. A kid named Marshall, who had a thick unibrow that stood out beneath his helmet, didn't have a defender within seven yards of him. He was basically all alone. As the throw left my hand, I could tell it might have been a half-foot too high and a bit too far out in front. But it was still a ball that Marshall should have had for lunch. Instead, the pass bounced off his hands.

I felt my heart sink as the football fell to the ground.

Pisano stared at me from the sideline, his arms out at his sides, mystified at why I hadn't thrown deep.

I pointed at my eyes, to let him know I'd seen something.

Maybe it was my adrenaline pumping, or maybe I was just angry at myself. But when Marshall returned to the huddle, I couldn't hold back.

"Come on, man. You should have caught that ball easy. We're trying to accomplish something here."

"My bad," he muttered.

I completed my next two passes but couldn't ditch the image of the dropped ball. Marshall had cost me a record that should have been mine.

Later, I found Marshall wide open. His defender had tripped. So he streaked straight downfield, waving at me, a good ten yards behind the rest of the defense. I lofted the ball up high into the lights and stars, like it might never come down.

When it did, it landed right in his arms for a score.

I ran full-speed to the end zone to celebrate.

"So you do have a pair of hands!" I hollered, slapping Marshall on the helmet.

He smiled and said, "I owed you one."

I wanted to tell him that he hadn't owed me anything. That my incomplete pass to him was a dud. But I just slapped the side of his helmet again and said, "Debt paid."

＊ ＊ ＊

Early in the fourth quarter, we were destroying Chiles 49–12. Pisano wanted to take me out of the game and let my new backup get some playing time. But I already had four touchdown passes, and a fifth would improve my state ranking big-time.

"Just one more series," I pleaded with Pisano. "I want to work on my timing with some of our second-stringers."

Pisano swallowed that line and let me back onto the field. On our next pass play, I had a receiver about to break open on a slant route. Holding the ball for an extra beat, I could sense the pocket starting to collapse around me and Chiles's D-line closing in quick. So I stepped forward to throw.

I released the ball clean. But on my follow-through, my elbow slammed against somebody's helmet.

The feeling was part intense pain and part tingling at first. Then the tingling stopped, leaving nothing but pain shooting up and down my left arm. I bolted to the sideline.

"Looks like you hit your humerus, the funny bone," our trainer said. "It's beginning to swell a little. We'll get an X-ray to be on the safe side."

After the game, Mom and him took me to the emergency room.

"If you're not crying, I don't think it's fractured," Mom said.

"I don't cry over anything," I told her. "Not anymore."

But I was paranoid, thinking the worst, like six weeks in a cast. I cursed myself for not letting Pisano take me out of the game. The only thing in my favor was that Beauchamp had a bye week coming up. Our next game wouldn't be for another fourteen days.

The doctor diagnosed the injury right away, after putting my X-ray up to a bright light: "Just a bruise and a slight ligament strain to the ulna. As far as football's concerned, you're either going to have to rest it or deal with the discomfort until it fully heals."

"Discomfort's not a problem. Neither is playing in pain," I said, with Mom giving me a look that told me a lecture was coming.

We got home just before midnight. Galaxy greeted us at the front door, jumping up for attention. I had to rub him under his neck using my right arm.

Mom tried to give me that *your health is more important than football* speech. But I let out a yawn and rubbed my eyes, using exhaustion as an excuse to duck it.

@TravisG_Gator *Beauchamp Bobcats 3-0. I'm ranked in the Top-10 QBs in FL again. This is either heaven or a great dream. Nobody pinch me.*

CARTER'S TAKE

Travis showed up at the complex Saturday morning with his left arm in a sling, asking Coach Harkey the best way to heal a bruised elbow. Coach didn't tell him anything I wouldn't have—heat, ice, rest, and the whirlpool. But what he told Travis about his long-range plans for him sent up some red flags for me.

"What you really need is more muscle on those bones," Harkey said. "That's something you and I will work on over time. Pads don't protect bones from breaking—flesh does. The more muscle tone you have, the healthier you'll stay playing this game, especially at quarterback."

"I get that just from lifting more?" Travis asked.

"That, and what you put into your body," Harkey said.

"I'm developing some new, high-protein shakes. I've used them with several Gators already. Turn you right around, into a Mr. Universe type. But that's way in the future for you."

That comment made me think about how much time Harkey had spent with Alex, going *beyond* blood, sweat, and tears. I'd never witnessed Coach H. do anything that wasn't on the up-and-up or even heard whispers from other players about it. But this was my baby brother, and I determined to keep my eyes wide open.

"Is that how you got those biceps to bulge?" Travis asked me.

"I wish it was that simple, bro. You've been through the workouts with us. You've seen what it takes."

"Your brother's a different animal, a different personality," said Harkey. "His body gains that mass just by doing the work. Then again, you've got those same genes."

"Yeah, but what about when you're injured?" Travis asked.

"I think Coach had it right from the beginning," I told Travis. "Stick with all the smart and simple things. You took that hit just last night. Your elbow will come around."

"I've only got two weeks," Travis said. "That's when we play Lincoln."

"You can't think that way," I told him. "Football shouldn't dictate your life."

Those words came out of my mouth real easily. But I understood exactly what Travis was feeling. I'd felt that way myself, maybe right up until the moment that Alex died.

THE GAINESVILLE SENTINEL

Section D/Sports – Columnists

GATORS GET OFF EASY THROUGH SELF-SCRUTINY

KAREN WOLFENDALE

The NCAA's Committee on Infractions announced yesterday its plan to impose a series of penalties on the Gainesville University football program. This comes in response to a pair of incidents in which past players received illegal benefits from boosters. The penalties include the loss of eight scholarships and eight practices across the next three seasons, a total only slightly greater than the university's proposed penalty of six scholarships and six practices. Other universities with similar problems, such as the University of Southern California, Ohio State, and Miami, had previously received stiffer punishments. The NCAA probe of the Gainesville football program began following reports that student-athletes had accepted cash payments from local boosters.

"We uncovered it, reported it, and addressed it. Now we'll move on," said Head Coach Elvis Goddard, who had already cut program ties with the boosters involved.

The university's internal investigation began after the NCAA's notice of an inquiry into charges made by several former players. NCAA members found insufficient evidence of payouts beyond one student-athlete accepting a discount on a flat-screen TV and a pair of student-athletes being overpaid for work as members of a restaurant waitstaff.

"I don't know why those former players made those claims," said Goddard. "Football is an extremely emotional game. There are hurt feelings everywhere. That will never change."

The Gators football program did not receive an NCAA ban on participation in post-season bowl games, which would have cost the university millions of dollars in revenue.

CHAPTER 21

The night after I hurt my elbow, the Gators hosted the University of Mississippi Rebels. About an hour before the game, Coach Goddard tapped me hello on the left arm. It hurt like anything. But I wouldn't even flinch, not wanting him to think I was the kind of quarterback who bellyached over every bump and bruise.

"Looking forward to another big win, Coach?" I asked.

With a hint of a smile, he answered, "At this level, no win's ever big enough. That's why I look back as much as I look forward. Think on that, Travis."

I tried, but I couldn't make any real sense of it.

The Gators' quarterback, Billy Nelson, was having problems with his accuracy all game. Watching from the sideline, I felt like I could have made most of his throws myself. Carter bailed him out twice by picking a pair of passes off his shoestrings before they skimmed the ground. But instead of being happy about it, Carter came off the field mad at himself for missing a blocking assignment. I hadn't noticed. I guess Coach G. didn't either, because all he said to Carter was, "Nice hands, Gardner."

The Gators beat the Rebels 32 to 18. Only, Carter didn't look pleased. I reminded him of the compliment he had gotten from Coach G., but he cut me off: "The coaches will catch that missed block on the game tape. They always do. And even if they don't, I'll know that I screwed up. That's enough for me."

* * *

Crystal was one of the prettiest cheerleaders at Beauchamp High—a tenth-grader with gorgeous green eyes that reminded me of a cat's. She'd flashed enough smiles in my direction that I felt confident asking her out.

"You free this Sunday?" I'd asked her, a few days before we'd drubbed Chiles.

Right away, she answered, "Sure, I'd like that."

I'll admit it—part of the reason why I asked was the chance to go out with a girl who was a year older. When I bragged about it to some of my teammates, one of them told me, "Crystal went out with Aiden Conroy a couple of times last year, before she dumped him."

That made the thought of going out with Crystal even sweeter.

I figured she'd probably dated juniors and seniors who had their driver's licenses. I didn't want to take her to a movie on the city bus. Or come off looking like a little kid by having Mom drive us. So when Carter came home to do his laundry, I asked if he wanted to do a double date in that sports car of his.

"I'm cramming for exams," Carter said, before breaking out in a big grin. "But exactly why would *I* take a girl out just to babysit the two of you?"

That's when I offered to wash all his filthy clothes as a trade.

"Think about it, Carter, because *I'm* not washing them," Mom said.

He still wouldn't do it.

"*Thanks*. Nice to know you're always there when I need you," I told him.

Later on, after Carter left, Mom cornered me and tried to have *the talk*.

"Travis, this is an older girl. I just want to make sure that you're ready for these relationships."

It was embarrassing. I never dreamed I'd hear something like that from her. I tried to cut her off short, but she kept at it. And deep down, I blamed Dad for putting me in that awkward position by not being there.

● ● ●

The morning of my date with Crystal, Mom let me put in a few hours at the dealership.

"I see you're dragging that left arm a bit," said Walter Henry, who still looked broken up over Alex, with heavy bags beneath his reddened eyes.

"Just nicked up. Nothing major," I said, not wanting to complain. So I changed the subject. Eventually, the conversation got around to Crystal and my lack of wheels.

"What time's your movie?" Walter asked.

"Four-thirty."

"Tell you what, I'll have a junior salesman take a car off the lot," he said. "He'll drop you and your date off at the theater. But you're on your own coming home. I close up early on Sundays."

"Really? That's unbelievable!"

"I assume you want a car that'll make the right impression."

"I owe you huge," I said, giving him an authentic Gator Pound. "Can I work a few extra hours for free to pay you back?"

"Forget it for now," Walter said.

"Hey, maybe you could be my agent one day," I said.

"It's a possibility," he replied. "That's where I was heading with Alex, until—"

He walked away before finishing, and I wouldn't touch the subject either.

◆ ◆ ◆

"This is great," Crystal said as our driver for the night opened the door of a cherry-red Benz. "How'd you swing it?"

"Just the perks of a part-time job at a dealership," I answered.

When we arrived at the theater, I made sure it was *me* holding the car door open for Crystal. I paid for our movie tickets too. Then, at the concession stand, I tried to order us a large popcorn and two sodas.

"Oh, I can't drink a whole soda," said Crystal. The heels on her suede boots made her almost as tall as me. "If it's all right, I'll sip from yours."

"No problem," I said.

The theater was pretty crowded, but we snagged two seats in one of the last half-empty rows up close to the screen. I made sure to sit on Crystal's left. That way, I could work on slipping my right arm around her without any stress on my sore elbow.

As the first preview started to play, I heard somebody call my name—PJ, a junior at Beauchamp and one of our buff linebackers: "Hey, Travis! Thanks for saving us seats, man."

Then PJ and his date started down our row.

When the girl with him raised her head, I saw it was Lyn.

I sat there motionless, like somebody had paused the DVR on my life.

"Lyn, this is my teammate Travis. And this is Crystal," PJ said. "You all know each other?"

Crystal answered something, but I don't remember what.

As PJ and Lyn settled in their seats, he gave her a quick kiss. I could feel my blood beginning to boil. Sweat started running down my forehead. I couldn't figure out why I was so upset. Lyn and me weren't officially dating, and I was there with Crystal. So I should've been able to say, "Whatever."

Once the movie started, Crystal snuggled up close to me. Only, I couldn't get my mind off Lyn being there with somebody else. I wanted to walk out right then. But that would be like giving Lyn some kind of victory.

An hour into the movie, I couldn't take it anymore.

I whispered to Crystal, "Let's get out of here. We can find better stuff to do."

She seemed confused, but she got up to follow me anyway.

"You guys leaving?" PJ asked in a low voice.

"Yeah, this movie really sucks," I said, with people around us telling me to *shush.*

After that, we went walking through the mall next to the multiplex for a while before getting something at Dave & Buster's. But I couldn't concentrate on the food or any of those games that I usually loved. And in the end, Crystal texted her mother to come pick us up.

◆ ◆ ◆

On Monday, Damon quit the team. I'd meant to text him, to find some time to learn what was going on with him. But things were so hectic, I never did. By the time I saw Damon leaving the locker room before practice, he'd already turned all his gear in to Pisano.

"I can't believe you're quitting. We're undefeated," I told him. "We dreamed about being Bobcats since Pop Warner. What's wrong?"

"Football doesn't mean something to me the way it used to," said Damon. "I'm more excited about body-building. I want to train for it without practice and games getting in the way."

I had to admit, Damon was looking great, almost nothing like Ground Round from middle school anymore.

"You can always be a Bobcat next year. If you get lean enough, maybe you can be one of my receivers."

"You never know," said Damon. "Playing together in the park all these years, I've probably caught more of your passes than anybody else."

I didn't throw during practice at all that week. But after seven days of heat balms, ice packs, and whirlpool dips, my left elbow started to feel much better. And I still had a solid seven days left until our game with the unbeaten Lincoln squad and its top-ranked defense.

"That Lincoln D will be our biggest test all season. They get physical as soon as they step off the bus," Pisano told me. "I want your elbow completely rested. I doubt you'll forget how to throw after a week off."

But one week was as long a stretch as I could

remember without a football spiraling out of my hand. So I wasn't totally sure.

* * *

The Gators played a nationally televised game that next Thursday night in South Carolina. Mom and me watched from home on ESPN. The Gamecocks were blazing fast, and the Gator offense really missed Alex's jets. Carter stepped up big, though. He ran one of the best routes I'd ever seen. South Carolina blitzed their linebacker, who'd normally be covering the Gators' tight end. That left Carter one-on-one with one of South Carolina's speedy defensive backs. Instead of trying to shake loose from that rabbit, my brother ran right at him. The defender had no choice but to backpedal. As soon as he did, Carter made his cut. Billy Nelson delivered the pass between the eight and the five on Carter's jersey.

Carter cradled the ball in his hands like it was a newborn baby, then turned into a steamroller, using his weight and momentum to run right over the Gamecocks' defensive back.

"Look who's got the hammer, defense!" Mom hollered at the screen. "Carter Gardner! That's who!"

"Tell 'em, Mom."

Gainesville won 23–13, improving their record to 4 and 0.

CHAPTER 22

After the game against South Carolina, Dad sent a text to me and Carter. With neither of us playing football over the weekend, Dad promised to deliver on that fishing trip he owed us.

"I'll fly into Florida early Friday night," Dad told me over the phone later on. "We'll hit the road right from there, and it'll be just us three for the next two days."

So Carter came to get me on Friday. He drove us back to his dorm room to hang out as we waited to go meet Dad at the airport. Out of nowhere, about an hour before Dad's plane was supposed to land, a huge thunderstorm hit.

"Think Dad's flight will be late?" I asked Carter, watching the lightning and driving rain through his dorm room window.

He looked out as the water streamed down the double pane and said, "If there's a way to get a trip delayed, Dad will find it."

"Maybe with the weather, they'll divert his flight to Atlanta. And there'll be some insurance convention going on," I joked.

I went to sit on Alex's bed, but Carter pitched a fit.

"Get off there, bro," he snapped. "Have some respect."

Carter hadn't been assigned another roommate. He'd been keeping Alex's bed made up perfect, with the sheets and blanket smoothed out and pulled tight at the corners.

"I just like to see it a certain way," Carter said, half apologizing. "I know, I don't even keep my own bed like that."

"It's okay," I said, not wanting to make a fuss.

By five o'clock, the rain eased up, and Dad's flight arrived on time. We picked him up at the airport. Then we all piled into Carter's car and headed down to Daytona Beach.

"You got *what* kind of deal on this car? Carter, that's almost too good to be true," Dad said, checking out all the dials on the dashboard.

"You've seen the guy," I told Dad, as I stretched out across both back seats. "He's the one with all those crazy car commercials we used to crack up over—Indiana Jones, *Star Wars*, Spider-Man."

"And he's letting you both work hours that fit your schedules?" asked Dad. "What's the catch?"

"No catch," Carter said, slowing down for a police

cruiser parked on the highway shoulder. "Walter Henry's a friend of the football program. They're called boosters. Alex introduced me."

"Sounds like someone you boys should stay close to. It could be a life-changing relationship."

"Definitely," Carter said.

● ● ●

We stayed overnight in a motel. There were just two beds in the room, so naturally, Dad got one of them to himself. Me and Carter kicked around a bunch of ways to decide who'd get the other bed. But neither one of us wanted to be the loser and sleep on the floor. So in the end, we decided to bunk together. Half the night, the two of us went back and forth with identical complaints: "Move over! You're not giving me enough room."

Early the next morning, we drove to the docks and boarded a fishing boat, a sixty-five-footer called the *Sea Spirit*. There were maybe fifty people on our trip. After an hour of skipping over waves, we reached the middle of the ocean, no land in sight. Once the boat's engines shut off and people got their lines into the water, I was amazed by the quiet. I did my fishing right-handed. But after a while, I stopped even thinking about my elbow.

Dad, Carter, and me stood at the rail, within five or six feet of each other. Stretches of ten or fifteen minutes passed when we didn't say a word. But it was a good silence. After a few hours, I felt closer to Dad and Carter than I had in a long time. Dad was the first one to catch a fish, a twelve-pound red snapper. He held it up with the sun glistening off its scales. A member of the crew filleted the fish for him and then stored it in an ice cooler.

Later on, Carter got a barracuda on his line. They're not good eating-fish—barracuda are all about the fight they give you trying to land them. Earlier in the day, one of them—maybe even the same barracuda—bit a fish on someone else's line in half. Carter fought it hard for twenty minutes, until he was almost at the point of exhaustion. But he finally got it onto the boat. It had to be the ugliest fish in the world, with a face like a demon and a row of razor-sharp teeth. Somehow, a crew member got the hook out of its mouth and then released it back into the water.

"That was a hell of a workout," Carter said before downing a bottle of spring water. "Now let him go test somebody else."

All the fish I caught were too small to keep, and I had to release them. But that didn't matter to me. I still had a great time. That night, we brought Dad's red snapper fillets to a restaurant that cooked them up for us. I swear it was the best-tasting fish I ever ate.

Before we went to bed, Carter got a call on his cell from Walter Henry, who was shooting a new commercial the next day at the dealership. Carter put him on speaker:

"The idea came to me a few hours ago," Walter said. "I'm going to take a portion of the profits on every car sold during the rest of this football season and donate it to a scholarship fund in Alex's name. I want you guys to be in the commercial. You just have to stand there tossing a football, wearing jerseys. I'll do the rest. It'll be a great tribute to Alex's memory. What do you say?"

We'd planned on spending the next day on the beach. But neither one of us wanted to miss out on a tribute to Alex—or disappoint Walter.

"An opportunity to be on TV without your helmets? I think you should do it," Dad said. "Let people see your faces for a change."

So we drove back to Gainesville early the next morning.

When we got to the dealership, we spotted Walter, dressed like Tarzan, wearing a flowing black wig and a brown loincloth. He was in incredible shape, showing off six-pack abs that made me think he'd been doing sit-ups for a week straight. Dad looked like an old man next to him, even though Walter wasn't that much younger. Carter introduced them, and the two shook hands.

"I'm so proud to be associated with your sons," Walter said. "I'm a businessman by trade. But I love sports, especially football. Maybe one day, I'll be an agent, helping young players secure their first pro contracts."

"You'd probably be sensational at it," Dad said. "I have so much respect for everything you've built here.

I'd love to see my boys learn something from you about marketing and business."

"It would be my pleasure," replied Walter.

Part of the dealership's front lot was done up like a jungle, with fake trees and vines hanging everywhere. Up close, everything looked totally plastic. But when the director let me look through the camera lens, it all seemed real.

Walter had even hired an animal trainer who had three huge gators in a pen.

A minute into the shoot, it was easy to see that the director didn't count for much. Walter Henry ran the show. He had me and Carter wearing orange jerseys, tossing a football back and forth. The trainer's job was to get those gators to come right up to us and open their mouths. That's when we were supposed to drop the ball and call for help.

The trainer had been feeding the gators hotdogs and marshmallows on the end of a long stick since the time we'd got there, so they wouldn't be hungry for football players. But when he released them from the pen and they flashed their teeth just a few feet from me, I didn't have to *act* scared.

Right on cue, Walter swung in on a fake vine to rescue us.

"Me, Tarzan. You, Gators," Walter said before looking into the camera. "Come to Gainesville Motors. I'll save you even more."

* * *

Midway through school the next day, Ms. Orsini called me into her office. I'd scored a D-minus on Mrs. Harper's math quiz, so I kind of knew what it was going to be about.

"I'm monitoring you in that class, Travis. I've asked Mrs. Harper to alert me to any potential problems," she said.

"That's so unfair. Will she notify you about the good stuff I do too?" I asked.

"Yes, absolutely," said Ms. Orsini. "Should she have? Did you score high on a different quiz or exam?"

"No, not really."

Even though I begged her not to, Ms. Orsini called Mom. Then she put me on the phone with Mom, so we could talk about it, though Mom was mostly yelling.

"Maybe I got too caught up in rehabbing my elbow," I said, as my only defense.

"You think so?" Mom said sarcastically. "D-minus? Travis, did you even *know* a quiz was coming?"

I didn't answer and just let Mom talk herself out, figuring I'd have enough time before I got home to think of the best thing to say.

CARTER'S TAKE

A dozen NCAA investigators were searching through my dorm room, tearing apart everything in sight. Coach G. stood in the hall with a huge checklist. But he wouldn't set foot inside my room.

In my wallet, an investigator found a bunch of $100 bills.

"Guilty!" he said. Then Coach marked my name off the list.

Another investigator grabbed my car keys and shouted, "Guilty!" in a voice even louder than the first one.

That's when I woke up with a start, trembling and soaked in sweat. I could barely breathe, staring into the shadows by Alex's bed.

It was the worst nightmare I'd ever had. I would have rather been falling forever into some bottomless pit or running through the hallways at school in my underwear, lost and late for a final exam. Those would have been sweet dreams compared to this one.

Somewhere inside that terrible scene, I had seen Alex sitting on his bed, watching everything. I was frantic, wrapped up tight inside my sheets, struggling to get free. But Alex was completely calm.

"It's not worth it, fam," he said. "None of it is."

After that, I had no plans of going back to sleep.

I couldn't do anything about giving back the car, because it was in Mom's name. But I swore on Alex's grave, I'd never take another dime from Walter or anybody else, even if I had to keep my hands buried inside my pockets.

CHAPTER 23

Leading up to our game against Lincoln, I started throwing the football during practice again. I felt a twinge deep in the elbow joint every time I released a pass. Only, I wouldn't tell anyone. I just dealt with it. I took care not to put any real mustard on my passes, though. I didn't need the extra strain.

Pisano didn't put up an argument over me going easy.

"You might only have a handful of big throws in you right now. Don't waste them," he told me. "Besides, you should save any pain for the game."

I didn't know how to explain it to him, but I was already there.

Cortez walked up to me after practice and asked, "How bad you hurt? The entire defense wants to know if we have to shut out Lincoln to win."

"I'm not hurt. Just getting over being sore," I told him.

"I've watched you sling a football for months now," said Cortez, moving a step closer. "You were throwing at fifty percent today, max. I hope you're holding something in reserve, because those soft passes won't get it done against Lincoln."

"Maybe Aiden Conroy will transfer back," I said, making sure to smile. "He's got a pretty strong arm."

"Think I'd rather lose with you than ever win with *him* again."

"I haven't lost yet."

"No. But that's when you see what somebody's really made of," Cortez said. "When it all goes wrong."

* * *

I saw Lyn in the cafeteria that day. She didn't mention anything about that night at the movies, and neither did I.

"Hey, Damon told me he felt better after talking to you," Lyn said. "Thanks for that."

"Yeah? I wasn't much help. He'd already quit."

"I think you were the only *real* connection he felt to the team," she said, taking a seat with an open spot next to it. "I'm pretty sure my brother felt like he'd be disappointing you."

"How?" I asked, grabbing the other seat. "We were hardly on the field together anymore."

"You two played together for what, five years? Damon's always been on the line protecting you," Lyn said. "I guess he thought that you were under a lot of pressure here. He didn't want to abandon you."

Until those words came out of Lyn's mouth, I hadn't seen it like that.

"I can take it. That's what quarterbacks do," I said. "But maybe I can help him train after my season's over. I learned some things from the Gators' strength coach about lifting weights the right way."

"He'd probably enjoy it," she said. "I think he's been feeling like you've got too much going on lately to hang with him."

"He's right," I said. "I haven't even had time to hang with myself."

I spent the rest of that lunch period with Lyn. I decided to leave football and dating completely out of the conversation. Instead, we talked about our classes, our teachers, and how she wanted to play softball for the Bobcats in the spring. Lyn had Mrs. Harper for math too. And we both started poking fun at her pointed hairdo.

● ● ●

That Friday night, we were playing Lincoln High at home. Both teams stood undefeated, us at 3-0 and them, 4-0. Lincoln was head and shoulders the best squad on our schedule. We'd beaten Eastside by five points, while Lincoln had routed them by thirty. The game was super-important because the winner would be a lock to host an opening-round playoff game on their own turf.

I'd never seen our stadium so packed or heard the Bobcat crowd get so loud. Somebody even told me the Alachua fire marshal was such a big Bobcats fan, he'd closed his eyes to the seating-capacity law.

The guys on Lincoln's defensive line looked like they belonged on a college team, standing tall and probably outweighing our O-line by ten to fifteen pounds per man.

Lincoln had an all-state senior linebacker named Brian Newser, nicknamed Newser the Bruiser. I watched him for a while during warm-ups. He was charging around like an absolute madman, slugging his own guys harder than I'd been hit all year.

I stopped staring at the Bruiser when *he* started glaring at *me*. I'd put on my best game face, with every ounce of swagger I could muster. I wanted Newser to see what Coach G. had seen in me—a quarterback who understood calmness and execution. But in the end, I felt more like that male poodle three doors down from our house, the one Galaxy had backed down in a staring contest.

"That Bruiser's a stud. Keep him in your sights," Cortez told me before Lincoln kicked off to us.

"Any advice?" I asked him.

"Don't let him get a clear shot at you. Duck and dive. And don't let him see that elbow's not right. He'll focus in on it first thing, even if he has to get flagged for a late hit. I know I would."

"So he's a thug in a helmet and pads," I said.

"That's what all defensive players are, especially when we get a shot at the quarterback," Cortez said.

My elbow was feeling better than I'd expected as I took the field. I prayed it wouldn't feel any worse after taking my first real hit. We started out with the ball on our own nineteen-yard line. At the line of scrimmage, I nearly stood on my tiptoes to see over those Lincoln giants. Pisano had scripted our first three plays in advance—all runs. I was fine with that and didn't even think about checking off to a pass. I handed the ball to our fullback without any pain. Then I watched the play develop from behind, away from the collisions and scrum. On guts alone, our fullback gained four yards, driving his legs forward and lowering his center of gravity once he'd met the pile.

"Way to be! We're the tougher team!" I said, clapping my hands together.

Our next play demanded a pitch-out to the halfback, who was supposed to run it wide around the right end. As I barked out signals, my eyes met the Bruiser's for a second. They were brown, fierce, and focused on the center of my chest, as if Newser could see right through it.

"Hut!" sprung from my vocal cords.

I pitched the ball, and our halfback sprinted to the right with it. But he met a wall of defenders not far from the line of scrimmage. So he reversed field and headed back in my direction. The Bruiser stayed hot on his tail, moving like a Mack truck in high gear.

Our tailback sprinted past me. Maybe it was stupidity on my part. Maybe I *wanted* to get broken into three pieces and sit on the sideline. But I had Alex's double-infinity drawn on my cleats and a perfect angle on the Bruiser. So I lowered my right shoulder and stuck it square into his midsection. The crowd let out a roar as my body shook from the collision. But that all-state linebacker flew back almost as far as I did.

"I'll meet you back here again, Gator Boy!" the Bruiser shouted.

As my teammates picked me up off the ground, I checked out every part of myself. Still all in one piece, even my left elbow.

"Travis, next time, just get out of the way," one of my O-linemen told me. "We can't afford to lose you."

I nodded at him and at Pisano, who was yelling the same thing from the sideline. But that block had me completely pumped.

Two plays later, I called my first pass in the huddle. I took the snap and then a quick three-step drop. My receiver turned open across the middle of the field. I released the ball nice and easy, without trying to overthrow it. Except for that twinge in my elbow joint, the pass felt good. I watched the ball spiral perfectly out of my hand. Only, I could see it slice through the air slower than usual.

Then, an instant before the ball reached my receiver, a defender cut in front of him and intercepted the pass. It felt like I'd been driving the Goodyear blimp over our stadium and the Lincoln D had let the air out. The defender returned it down to our seventeen-yard line. And I walked off the field looking at my left arm, wondering where the strength had disappeared to.

The Lincoln offensive line loomed as large as its D. On their first play from scrimmage, two linemen double-teamed Cortez and blocked him onto his back.

After that, Lincoln marched the ball down our throats for a 7–0 lead.

Pisano had called some conservative plays, probably because of my arm. And I was being careful to not leave the ball hanging out there. But after Lincoln scored another touchdown, on a play where their running back knocked over Cortez and another one of our defenders like they were bowling pins, that changed. We had to open up our offense to try and stay within reach. That meant using routes that stretched their defense.

By the second quarter, I was throwing my passes harder and harder, trying to get more zip on them. But no matter how much pain I withstood, my passes didn't have enough velocity. And the more I put into them, the more they started to stray offline.

I had a receiver open on a deep slant and a wide five-yard window in which to deliver the ball. My eyes lit up at the sight of it. But when I tried to muscle it there, the ball sailed on me, and I got intercepted for a second time.

I was almost completely deflated. And it wasn't just me, either. Lincoln had outplayed us in every phase of the game.

We headed to the locker room, down 24–0.

Our once-rocking stadium sounded more like a graveyard now, and lots of Bobcats had their heads down.

"If you're going to get your butts whipped, at least keep your heads up! That way you can see it coming!" Pisano exploded in our locker room. "This second half isn't about winning and losing now. It's about who's ready to be a man and who's not!"

Cortez had his defense huddled in the corner. He pointed at himself for not getting it done. I wasn't sure what to say to my receivers. Finally, I looked at them and said, "Just keep getting open."

Early in the third quarter, the Bruiser knocked our best running back out of the game, dropping him like a bag of crushed ice. Without him to worry about, Lincoln started blitzing me on every play. That meant seven defenders were trying to steamroll me into the ground. Twice, I swear the stadium lights disappeared as the pocket collapsed and Lincoln's defensive line swallowed me alive.

The pressure was unreal. I could barely get the ball

out of my hand, even to throw it away. Every time I got knocked to the ground, I had to focus on protecting my elbow as much as trying to complete a pass. And I knew my state QB ranking was taking a big hit too.

Deep down, I hoped Pisano would pull me from the game. He never did.

Late in the final quarter, we had a fourth down and two yards to go at midfield. Pisano wouldn't punt the ball back to Lincoln. He probably didn't want them scoring on us again. So he signaled for me to stay on the field and go for the first down.

Pisano sent in a dive play, with our replacement running back taking the ball right into the teeth of the defense. That was fine with me. But at the line of scrimmage, our center went brain-dead and snapped the ball at my feet. On instinct, I dove for it—along with half the Lincoln defense.

It was like outracing a bunch of jackals to a single piece of meat, even though I had no hunger left in me. I got to the football first and tucked it beneath me when the Bruiser slammed into my left elbow. A bolt of pain shot through my entire body. Then it happened again and again as other players piled on top, some of them Bobcats.

I almost cursed Damon for that miserable snap. Then I remembered he didn't play football anymore. The ref found me at the bottom of the pile with the ball clutched to my chest, and Lincoln took over on downs.

We lost, 38 to 6. My elbow throbbed nonstop for the next seven hours. Once I got home, I took two Tylenol out of our medicine chest and swallowed them down, without telling Mom about the pain or those pills.

@TravisG_Gator *My 1st loss in a HS uni. Bad taste in my mouth.*

CHAPTER 24

By Saturday night, I'd taken enough Tylenol that I had to go out and buy another bottle. I couldn't risk Mom going into the medicine chest and discovering we were almost out. I skipped work at the dealership that day so I could ice my elbow while Mom was out of the house.

Carter and the Gators were in South Bend, Indiana, for the weekend to play the Fighting Irish of Notre Dame. That meant I couldn't get any help from Harkey with my elbow. I stayed in my room most of the day, resting it. I told Mom I was working on a project for school. She even brought dinner to me on a tray when I didn't come out to eat.

"Don't tell me you're going to watch the game in here tonight," Mom said. "I like having someone to root with."

"I just have to finish what I'm doing," I said, pointing at some unfinished homework assignments on my desk.

"Are you sure you're not feeling blue over losing yesterday?" she asked. "You don't look like the Travis I know. You're looking a little defeated."

"It was just one game," I said. "Honestly, I'm more worried about next week."

Mom kissed me on the forehead.

"You feel a little warm. You might be running a slight fever. Keep an eye on that, all right?" Mom said as she left my room.

"I will."

Carter played a sensational game that night. He had four receptions in the first half. The TV analyst even called him "an emerging pro prospect."

I heard those words before Mom did, because she was watching in HD, which has about a two-second delay.

"Listen for it!" I screamed to her.

"That's my oldest boy!" Mom hollered after she'd caught up. "Air high five on that one, Travis!"

"You got it!" I yelled back.

But my elbow was wrapped up in a heating pad. So I left Mom hanging out there, even if she didn't know it.

The Gators pummeled the Fighting Irish, 38 to 9.

* * *

Dad didn't call me Saturday. I hadn't heard from him since our fishing trip. I left him a message on Sunday, but he never phoned back.

I went to school the next day with my elbow aching unless I held it completely still. They served pizza in the cafeteria for lunch. That was good for me. I could fold over a slice and eat with just my right arm.

I started to dread the idea of going to practice. I knew Pisano would be riding us hard over getting blown out. But once I got there, to my surprise, he pushed everybody to the limits with extra drills except me.

"Nothing but short, easy tosses for a few days," Pisano told me, once he'd stopped screaming at the team. "That funny bone's a tricky thing. I want it to be stronger for the Orange Park game."

"That's the life of a quarterback," Cortez said back in the locker room. "We win, he gets girls wearing his jersey. He throws interceptions, we do punishment pushups."

And to a man, everyone who heard him agreed.

◆ ◆ ◆

Two days later, report cards for the first marking period came out. Only, a parent had to come to open-school night to pick it up.

I walked through the main entrance that night with Mom. We stopped at the guidance office first, to see Ms. Orsini and get my report card. I figured I had done okay in my classes. Still, it felt like torture, not knowing my grades and having to bring Mom along. There wouldn't be enough time for her to digest any bad news before she met my teachers.

"Ms. Gardner, we've spoken before. What a pleasure to meet you in person," Ms. Orsini said, smiling and shaking Mom's hand. "I want you to know it's wonderful to see Travis every day. Besides being his guidance counselor, I'm his US History teacher. I'm really pleased with the attitude he brings to class. In fact, I think being a football fan has given him some unique knowledge."

I wanted to hug Ms. Orsini for saying that, and I started to breathe a little easier.

"Well, that's a surprise to hear," Mom said, with a widening smile.

"That's right. You know that team, the Oklahoma Sooners?" I asked Mom, who nodded her head. "They get their name from the Land Rush of . . . uh . . . uh . . ."

Ms. Orsini filled in the blank for me: "Eighteen eighty-nine."

"Yeah, that's why they're called the Sooners. They snuck onto the land *too soon* to claim it," I said with confidence, like I'd made the right audible at the line of scrimmage.

"Let me give you Travis's report card," Ms. Orsini said, finding it in a stack of them. "I gave Travis a B-plus in my class, so there's still room for improvement. His other grades this semester are good, except for math, where he seems to have some personal conflict with the teacher."

I looked over Mom's shoulder to find my cumulative average at the bottom. It was a B. I could have done a touchdown dance right then. Next, I searched for Ms. Harper's math grade: a C-minus.

"I've heard about it from Travis. I'll be sure to speak with her tonight," Mom said.

"I also wanted to comment on Travis's ability to handle everything that's been put in front of him," Ms. Orsini said. "He seems to be doing an incredible job with all of it—the pressure of living up to his scholarship, media attention, his popularity here, his studies. It can't be as easy as it looks, Travis. Can it?"

"Gets hard sometimes," I answered, trying to sound humble.

"It has to be, right?"

"I know. I worry about him dealing with so much," Mom said, squeezing my left arm.

I had to clench my teeth to keep from screaming out in pain.

"Travis, promise us when that weight gets too heavy, you'll talk to your mother and me," Ms. Orsini said. "It's not something you need to handle alone."

"I will. I promise," I said, slipping free from Mom's grasp.

"Remember, you're a quarterback, not a superhero," said Mom.

"You're also a teenager," Ms. Orsini added, walking us toward the door, where another kid and his parents were waiting to see her. "Sometimes that can be the most difficult part."

After we left there, I wanted Mom to visit Coach Pisano next. He took special care of his players and had given me an A-plus in PE. All I really had to do for him was not cut class and keep my gym clothes from reeking. I'd earned that privilege on the football field. I knew everything Pisano could possibly say about me would be positive. But Mom was headed to Mrs. Harper's room, not to Coach Pisano's, and I couldn't stop her.

"For some reason, I can't picture Mrs. Harper in my mind," Mom said as we walked. "I remember Carter having her more than once. *He* didn't have any problems. I think he got As in her class."

"She's older now and probably losing it," I said. "She hates that I have a scholarship already, thinks it's some kind of free ride I don't deserve."

"Everyone knew your brother would get a football scholarship. She didn't have a grudge against *him*," Mom said.

I shook my head, as if Mom hadn't heard a word out of my mouth.

Mom wrote her name and mine on the sign-in sheet by Mrs. Harper's door. Then she walked around the classroom, looking at some of the perfect test papers hanging up on the walls, while Mrs. Harper talked to another parent. If Mom was expecting to see any of my papers there, she wasn't going to find one.

Mrs. Harper had dressed up for the night, and she'd used more hair spray than usual. She looked like Wolverine's grandmother had dressed up for an old folks' dance, with her hair pointier than I'd ever seen.

"Still can't picture her?" I whispered to Mom, who shot me a glare.

As Mrs. Harper finished with the parent and kid ahead of us, she pulled out a quiz our class had taken that afternoon. I couldn't believe she'd graded it so fast. Didn't she have any kind of life?

"Mrs. Gardner, hello." Mrs. Harper waved Mom up to her desk. "I'm ready for you now. Please be seated."

I stood beside Mom, wanting to stay light on my feet in case metal claws popped out from Mrs. Harper's knuckles and she tried to slice me.

"If you look at your son's test scores, you'll see exactly why I gave him a C-minus," she said, showing Mom her marking book. "His highest grade is a B, and his lowest is a D-minus."

"Travis seems to feel that you have something personal against him and his athletic success," Mom said, flat out.

"On the contrary. What I have is a *personal interest* in him, along with every other student in my charge. I have to ensure that your son gets treated the same as everyone else, regardless of his other pursuits."

"I don't believe Travis is looking for special treatment," Mom said.

"Good, he'll only get what he deserves in my class," Mrs. Harper shot back, as I started to feel like a ping-pong ball. "I'm solely here to teach."

She passed the quiz from that afternoon to Mom. There was a C on top of the paper. I was almost relieved.

"Apparently you don't understand *absolute value*," said Mrs. Harper, pointing to a particular problem on my paper. "I'm surprised, because I called you up to the board last week to look at exactly this."

"What's wrong with this answer?" I asked. "Four's worth more than negative four. Everybody knows that."

Even Mom was nodding her head in agreement.

"Well, on the number line, they're both four places away from zero," Mrs. Harper answered. "They're exactly equal. When it comes to absolute values, there are no negatives."

"I see," said Mom, sounding schooled.

After that, Mom sat down with me almost every night to go over my math homework.

* * *

I left Dad another message when we got home from open-school night. Only, he didn't get back to me until the next day, late on Thursday night. When he did, I could hear the stress in his voice.

"Sorry I haven't called. I just got a new apartment," he said. "It's been so hectic. There are cardboard boxes everywhere."

"What do you mean, *apartment*? I thought you lived in a house," I said, sitting on my bed watching *SportsCenter*.

"I need to tell you something. I'm separated from Heather now," he said. "It all fell apart fast. That's how it goes sometimes in relationships."

"When are you coming back to Florida?"

"Well, I won't get a real vacation for another—"

"I don't mean on vacation," I said. "I mean to *live*. If you're not with Heather, there's no reason to be in California."

"Son, this is where all my business is," he said. "I can't leave my clients behind and start from nothing again. I'm too old for that. Now that I'm single, maybe you can come out here for an extended visit."

"That's all right, I get it. Stupid me," I said, hanging up. I punched the nearest pillow enough times that Galaxy came running into my room to investigate. And for a while after that, I hardly noticed my elbow. I guess a few hours passed until it ached more than the rest of me.

THE GAINESVILLE SENTINEL

Section D/Sports – Columnists

TOP PROSPECT

KAREN WOLFENDALE

This is the second in a series of articles looking at the life of top prospect Travis Gardner as he advances along his trek from freshman year of high school to a football scholarship at Gainesville University.

It's fifty-five degrees in Orange Park, chilly for October. Freshman quarterback Travis Gardner blows into his throwing hand, working to keep it warm, and then tosses a football on the sideline. Though this is a road game for the Beauchamp Bobcats (3-1), it isn't exactly hostile territory for Travis. The Orange Park Broncos are winless on the season (0-5), and many people here have packed the stands to see Coach Elvis Goddard's project-in-the-making.

Travis sports a small cut on his chin, though not from his first loss as a high school quarterback, an ugly defeat at the hands of highly ranked Lincoln High. Rather, it's from one of Travis's first attempts at shaving.

"I just need more practice time, more reps. I'll get better at it," Gardner joked.

The Broncos appear energized by the attention a visiting player has commanded on their home field. In response, the team executes a seventy-yard double-reverse for the game's opening touchdown, the Broncos' longest play from scrimmage all season.

"Our turn now. We'll get that score right back," Gardner tells his teammates.

The Bobcats' offense makes small gains throughout the first half. Travis's rifle arm and deep throwing ability are not on display. Instead, Coach Adam Pisano elects to feature his team's running game, along with an array of screens and short passes.

When Orange Park opens up a 14–0 advantage, the crowd wavers between wanting to witness the Broncos' first win or see Travis light up the scoreboard.

"Come on! Do something, Gardner!" moaned one Orange Park resident. "Borrr-ing!"

Undeterred, Travis executes the conservative Beauchamp game plan, leading his team to a much-needed score moments before halftime.

"We'll open things up more. We're just getting started," Gardner says before heading to the locker room.

The wind increases in the second half, and the temperature drops a few more degrees. Beauchamp attempts to open up its offensive attack, especially after the Broncos record another lightning-quick touchdown, extending their lead to 21–7.

"You have to stop these guys! You're making it too easy for them!" Gardner tells his defense.

That criticism ignites a brief but heated exchange between Travis and several of the Bobcats' senior defensive players. Though blowups are common among teammates, this one invites a larger question: Can a freshman lead upperclassmen through adversity?

"I've been under a microscope for a while. I'm used to it," Gardner said before game time.

In the third quarter, Travis fades back to launch a long bomb. The quarterback doesn't sense an Orange Park defender closing in on him from his blind side. Travis loses his grip upon impact and fumbles the football away.

A hard blow can disrupt a quarterback physically and mentally. After that big hit, Travis can't restart his passing game, despite opportunities at open receivers downfield.

"Honestly, I don't see what all the fuss has been about," says one fan. "Gardner looks like a normal freshman, some good plays followed by some bad ones."

When the clock runs out on Travis and his teammates, Orange Park wins 28–7.

"It's a disappointing loss, for sure," Gardner says. "I can't remember the last time I dropped two straight games. We have to get over it and beat Citrus next week. That's all I can focus on right now."

Frustrations rise among several Bobcats, who argue with each other as they board the team bus. But Travis, whose arm is already wrapped in ice, steers clear of any further conflict.

Without traffic, it's a ninety-minute ride back to Alachua.

Sometimes no bus is big enough for a football team that has just lost a game it was supposed to win. That's probably true for the Bobcats, who appear to be going through an intense case of growing pains.

CHAPTER 25

The morning after our game against Orange Park, I had to buy a second bottle of Tylenol. Before going down to the football complex to see Harkey, I popped a pair of pills in case he needed to touch my elbow. I texted Carter that I was coming, and for some reason, he insisted on meeting me. He was pedaling away on one of the complex's stationary bikes when I walked in.

"Your elbow's *still* sore?"

"I wouldn't say sore," I said. "Stiff, maybe. You hear about Dad?"

"Yup, he called me two nights ago, right after he spoke to you," Carter said, slowing down his RPMs.

"Surprised he's not moving back to Florida?" I asked.

"Nope. Not at all."

"How come?" I asked, with Harkey heading in our direction.

"Because I stopped believing in fairy tales," Carter answered. "I already learned the hard way."

"So tell me what's happening. Stiffness in the joint?" Harkey asked me, cupping my elbow in his palm once he reached us. "More so in the morning when you first get up?"

"Yeah, that's right."

"Any of this hurt?" he asked, manipulating it.

"Not really," I answered, trying hard not to wince.

"It's probably just some mild tendonitis," Harkey said. "Not unusual for a quarterback to have. The elbow joint wasn't designed to fire a football forty yards. But the more muscle you build, the more padding you'll have against these hits."

"I used to get that same stiffness," Carter said. "I started doing a rock climber's exercise for it. Here, put your arm out straight and bend the wrist back for a count of ten." He climbed down off the bike to demonstrate. "It builds up the forearm and takes pressure off the elbow."

"Actually, that's a very good exercise," Harkey said. "Try that five or six times a day for a few weeks. Then let me know how it's feeling."

"Okay, but you don't have any *special* exercises? Or supplements I can take?" I asked Harkey. "Like you did with Alex, when he was rehabbing his knee."

"No, this is simple ABC stuff. Stick with that stretch. If you're still sore after the season, once you've rested it, you may have a more serious problem. Then we'll address it together," Harkey said, heading toward the door. "I've got to move. There are some things I need to check on before the game tonight."

As Harkey left, I grabbed a Gatorade from a small refrigerator.

"You want one?" I asked Carter.

He shook his head and took a swig from a bottle of water hanging from the bike.

"Hey, Trav, fill me in on anything Harkey ever gives you—new exercises, vitamins, anything like that."

"Sure, but why?"

"I'll probably major in physical education. I could be a coach or a trainer one day. Observing Harkey could be good experience for me. Besides, there are no secrets between brothers, right?"

"I'm down with that. Fam all the way," I said.

★ ★ ★

That night, the Alabama Crimson Tide rolled into Gainesville. The Crimson Tide was one of the elite teams in the nation, and a win could clinch Gainesville a number-one ranking. 'Bama had won the National Championship a few seasons back, earning a crystal football. In a crazy accident, some player's father bumped the table the football had been resting on while trying to take a photo with it. The trophy fell and smashed into a million pieces. The athletic department wouldn't give out the guy's name. That was probably a smart move, because Crimson Tide supporters are as insane for their team as Gator fans.

Defenses on both teams dominated from the start. It was a low-scoring game—and really physical too. Carter had to throw more blocks than running pass routes.

"Going undefeated is a test of fortitude. You have to win them all to play for it all," Coach G. told his players at the half. "Who are you going to be in life—a champion or an also-ran? The margin that separates the two can be razor-thin."

The Gators had the lead midway through the fourth quarter when Alabama finally punched one into the end zone to forge ahead, 7–3.

I didn't care how good the defenses were playing. Football is an offensive game. You can only win by putting points on the scoreboard. As far as I was concerned, both quarterbacks—the one in red and the one in blue—were dogging it.

With a little more than two minutes remaining, the Gators' D stripped the ball away and recovered it on the 'Bama nine-yard line. I could feel tremors from the crowd's stamping feet.

"That's the break we needed!" Carter hollered, strapping on his helmet and heading back onto the field. "Let's capitalize!"

The Gators prepared to bring 'Bama to the bottom of the mud in a death roll. I wished I could be out there at quarterback, leading them. But all I could do was cheer.

My elbow twinged as Billy Nelson released a first-down pass to one of his wide receivers. Incomplete, overthrown by a mile.

That's his nerves. He needs to settle down. Where's the calmness and execution? I thought.

Coach G. must have been thinking the same thing, because he sent in a running play next. The Gators pounded the ball down to the four-yard line, with their fullback scratching and clawing for every extra inch he could get.

Now Gainesville had two downs left to score. A stillness came over the stadium, from the air to the ground. But my heart was beating hard.

On third down, I watched Nelson's eyes as he dropped back to pass, searching right and then left. The Crimson Tide defense had Carter completely covered—he couldn't get himself free. Neither could anyone else. A look of panic crossed Nelson's face before his throw burrowed into the turf.

At fourth down, Coach Goddard wasn't interested in a field goal.

"Champions score touchdowns from here," he bellowed. "That's us. Go for it."

Carter exploded off the line of scrimmage at the first "Hut." He shed his defender with a swim move, circling one arm over the other, and then turned open in the end zone. But Nelson never saw him. His eyes were locked onto another receiver. I wanted to grab the ball out of the QB's hand and deliver it to Carter myself.

The pass went way wide. The receiver dove for the ball, but he didn't come within three feet of it. Carter fell down to one knee, covering his face mask with both hands, while the Crimson Tide defense celebrated.

Alabama took over, and the Gators never got another chance. So I tweeted exactly what I felt and hit Send.

@TravisG_Gator *<3-brking loss. If U want a ring QB can't pass that bad. Choked on final play.*

CARTER'S TAKE

I sat at my locker, trying to deal with the loss to 'Bama. Every part of me was hurting, inside and out. We'd flushed our entire season down the toilet—that's how it felt. More than anything, I tried not to focus my anger at Billy for failing to find me in the end zone.

Then, suddenly, *he* was in *my* face.

"Tell your loudmouth brother I'll knock him from here to tomorrow!"

"What are you blabbering about?" I shouted, with my forehead jutting till it nearly touched his.

"His tweets, Carter! His stupid tweets!"

A couple of our teammates separated us. Once I was clear, one of them held out his phone. He was about to show me what my brother had tweeted when Travis walked into the locker room.

Billy broke free from the guys holding him back and headed straight for Travis. I bolted there too, intercepting him before he reached my brother.

"Back off!" I screamed, shoving Billy away. The two

of us almost came to blows over it, as I shielded Travis behind my body.

Coach G. came charging out of his office.

"If either one of you picks his hands up, it'll be the last thing you do as a Gator!" he shouted. Everything except my emotions came to an instant halt.

Travis stayed behind me, completely shook. He honestly looked like he had no idea what was going on.

"Let me see that phone," Coach G. said.

As he read the tweet, I could see the veins in his neck bulge. He turned a bright red. I was actually scared for Travis and what might happen next.

Coach G. raised his head and then shoved the phone back at the player who'd given it to him. "This is our publicity department's fault, not anyone's here. I'll take care of this. Meanwhile, I don't need to see or hear any more from my players on it. Shake hands and bury it right now. And If the press gets word of this little spat, you'll *all* have to deal with me."

Then Coach G. marched into his office to make a phone call.

After I finally read the tweet, I understood what all the fuss had been about. But a few minutes later, without Travis doing a thing, that tweet had magically changed to something more positive.

When everything had calmed down, I made sure that Travis apologized to Billy one-on-one. Because if somebody around our squad had tweeted that first message about me, I would have wanted to confront him too.

Later on, I told Travis, "You better learn what it means to be a good teammate. How not to point that finger of blame."

"Why? I face it all the time as a quarterback," he said.

"Believe me, Trav. You may not see it, but more people have your back than you realize."

CHAPTER 26

All day Sunday, I put up with pain in my elbow. On top of that, my stomach ached. I felt nauseous, probably from all the Tylenol.

NFL games were on at one, four, and 8:30 p.m., but I didn't turn on the TV or check any of the scores. I used to watch every play of every game religiously with Carter and my friends. We'd polish off big bags of Doritos and down a few gallons of Sunny D. During halftime, we'd go outside and toss a football, reenacting the game highlights. That was some of the most fun I ever had. But things had changed. I lived and breathed football 24/7.

Dad called me around nine. I remembered what Carter had said about not believing in fairy tales. So I decided to cut Dad some slack over staying in Los Angeles. But as soon as I did, his latest update slapped me in the face.

"Here's the new plan. I'm very excited about it," Dad said. "I'm moving down to San Diego next month. There are a lot more opportunities there in the insurance field. The weather's absolutely beautiful. It's always—"

"Wait, let me get this straight," I said. "You're changing cities. You're starting your business over from *nothing*. But you're not coming back to Florida to do it?"

"I thought we'd been through this already, Travis."

"We have. And you know what? Don't come back," I said. "Living in Cali, there are fewer chances for you to disappoint me."

"Travis, I can hear how—"

I didn't let him finish.

Dad called me back within five minutes. Only, I wouldn't pick up, and I wouldn't listen to the voice mail he left either.

● ● ●

On Monday, I got to the cafeteria a minute before the changing bell rang. As kids in the lunch period ahead of mine got ready to leave, I grabbed a seat at Lyn's usual table, shoving aside a dirty lunch tray.

"Mr. Gardner, *every* student at Beauchamp is responsible for his or her own garbage. Please dispose of that tray properly."

It was Mrs. Harper. I guess she had agreed to do lunch duty for an absent teacher, because I'd never seen her patrolling the student cafeteria before.

She stood next to my chair, looking down at me.

"It's not mine," I said. "I just got here."

"I saw you touch it, Mr. Gardner," she said. "That makes it yours."

When Mrs. Harper's fingers landed on the edge of the table, I pushed the tray against them.

"There, now *you* touched it," I said. "It must be yours. Throw it out."

"That will earn you a detention slip."

"I figured Wolverine's grandma would like going through the garbage."

I was so mad I hadn't even noticed that Lyn showed up.

"Travis, calm down. Before you get suspended," Lyn said, getting between me and Mrs. Harper. "*I'll* throw out the stupid tray."

Mrs. Harper finally walked away, and I figured that was that. But a few minutes later, Ms. Orsini came and took me to her guidance office.

"Travis, what happened?" Ms. Orsini asked. "Did you really do what Mrs. Harper's claiming?"

I explained the whole situation. But the more I talked, the more she looked disappointed in me.

"You're going to need to apologize to Mrs. Harper," she said.

"For what? Not letting her push me around?" I stormed out of Ms. Orsini's office, kicking a chair outside her door.

The school called Mom, and when I got home, she scolded me for a half-hour straight. I'd calmed down a lot by then, and just let her go off on me.

In the end, I had to apologize to Mrs. Harper, in person and in writing, to not be suspended. I wound up apologizing to Ms. Orsini too, because I wanted to.

"My temper just ran away with me," I told her. "I'm really sorry. You're my favorite teacher."

"Thank you," Ms. Orsini said. "We all lose it sometimes. Now you have to look in the mirror and ask yourself, why?"

I thought it could be my elbow pain or the pressure of playing losing football. But that wasn't about to come out of my mouth.

"I'm not sure. I was having an okay day up until then," I said.

"Well, when you figure it out, I'm always here to listen," she said.

I should have told her about Dad staying in California. At least I could have gotten that off my chest.

CHAPTER 27

Pain didn't matter to me anymore. I needed a win in the worst way. Another loss and I'd be three and three as a high school quarterback, nothing but average. The rest of our guys were feeling the pressure too. But I had a special kind of stress to deal with, since Aiden Conroy had become the starting quarterback for our next opponent, Citrus High.

"We'll use our normal audibles—tango, bravo, and Omaha," Pisano explained at practice. "But each one will mean something different now. Whatever Aiden told the Citrus coaching staff about our offensive keys will come back to bite them."

"Then we can change those audibles back and really mess with their minds," I said.

"You're beginning to learn how the game works," said Pisano. "Just make sure it doesn't work *you*. Don't let your emotions take over your judgment out there."

"I'm definitely hyped to outplay him," I said.

"Remember, you have a whole team behind you.

Everyone needs to carry part of the load. Your shoulders aren't that wide, not even in pads."

On Thursday, I took three Tylenol just to practice. Before warm-up exercises, Cortez and a few other guys on our defense came up to me.

"Everything's buried from last week, all the arguing and bad feelings," Cortez said, with his brothers on D agreeing. "This is *one* team with *one* goal: win tomorrow night. We're going to carry you there if we have to."

"Don't worry. I'll use my own two legs," I said, giving each guy a pound. "But if you're going to give me an extra push, I'll take it."

Mom sat shotgun as I did my homework that night. I had a science quiz the next day on the periodic table of elements. I almost got a migraine headache trying to memorize all of the symbols. To me, it looked like an uneven football field, with the table's boxes being the yard markers. There was even a red zone at one end of it.

"You really look out of it," Mom said. "Why don't you take some aspirin?"

I shook my head. The periodic table's symbols were way more complicated than my wristband of football plays. And I went to bed cursing whoever invented such a stupid thing.

Lying between my sheets, I couldn't get comfortable. I was concentrating on keeping my weight off my left arm. Then, the thought of losing to Aiden started creeping in. I imaged having to shake his hand at midfield after the game. But every time my hand was about to touch his, I scrubbed the image from my mind.

I eventually lay flat on my back, with my elbow on a pillow. The blanket began to feel heavy on my chest, making it hard to breathe. So I tossed it. I'm not sure when I finally fell asleep. I remember sweating a lot. I woke up almost an hour before my alarm went off, with my mouth feeling drier than a desert. Only, I was too exhausted to get up for a glass of water. And I spent the rest of the time staring at the clock, watching the lighted numbers change.

* * *

School that Friday was mostly a blur to me. Everybody wanted to talk about the game. I'd just smile and shut out their words. On my science exam, I knew to write *Te* when I saw *tellurium* because Carter was a tight end—TE. And I knew to write *Fe* when I saw *iron*, because Alex played ball at Santa *Fe* High. I wished the periodic table had a QB element, but there wasn't one. During math, I kept my eyes glued to my notebook. I doodled at the top of the page, refusing to even look at Mrs. Harper.

I sat on the side during Pisano's PE class with my face buried inside our playbook, even though half the time my eyes were shut trying to catch up on lost sleep.

Mom came home early from work that day and made sandwiches for dinner. She put a fresh-cut roll on my plate and then laid out sliced turkey, ham, olive loaf, and cheese in the middle of the table so I could make my own hero.

"Sorry we don't have everything here to make an official Travis G. Gator," Mom said, still wearing her green hygienist's outfit.

"That's all right," I said, as Mom sat down across from me. "I've had my fill of those. I don't really like provolone."

I picked out every olive inside the olive loaf and piled them on a napkin.

Mom shook her head. "I don't know why you ask me to buy that, Travis. Without the olives, it's the same as bologna, only more expensive."

"I like the taste they leave behind," I said, putting potato chips on top of the meat. Then I closed the bread and listened for the crunch before deciding which flavor Gatorade I wanted.

"How's your elbow feeling?"

"Fine," I answered, making sure to twist off the cap with my left arm. "Not even tender anymore."

"Think you're going to win tonight?" she asked, spreading mayo over her bread and not the turkey.

"*Think?*" I said. "I *know* I'm going to win."

"Well, win or lose, you're still my son."

"Yeah, I know that too. That's cool for birthday cards," I said. "Not for talk before a football game. Besides, wouldn't you rather have a son who's a *winner?*"

"Yes. But to me, that's determined by the decisions you make *off* the football field."

All I could do was nod my head. Before I left the house, I went to my underwear drawer and swallowed some Tylenol. Just two pills, though. I put another two into my pocket. My plan was to take them in a couple of hours, right before kickoff.

*   *   *

During the warm-ups, Aiden got booed by the Beauchamp student body. On the field, he kept his mouth shut and acted like our guys didn't exist. But plenty of Bobcats had something to say to him. Guys on our offensive line called him a traitor. And before the game, some guys on the Bobcat defense put a bounty on Aiden. They'd kicked in twenty bucks each, ready to give the whole pot to whoever laid the hardest lick on him.

Citrus High won the coin toss and took the football first. For the moment, the pressure was off me. It was on Aiden to try and score, and on our defense to stop him. On Aiden's first pass attempt, our D-line chased him out of the pocket, running him down from behind. I started clapping. The crowd let out an extra cheer when Aiden got off the ground with a big clod of dirt and grass dangling from his face mask.

Our defense forced Citrus to punt, going three-and-out. Once the Bobcats had possession, I took a deep breath and jogged onto the field.

Pisano called for a screen pass to one of our running backs. I floated him the football without any *real* pain. Next came a short pass to a receiver in the flat, just five or six yards downfield. I connected on that too, giving us a first down. After that, our fullback exploded up the middle for a fifteen-yard run. The crowd was completely stoked.

I started barking out our normal audibles at the line of scrimmage, the ones Aiden must have told their coaching staff about.

"Bravo! Three fifty-four!" I hollered.

Citrus had been in a good defensive set to begin with. But their players started shifting all over the place, expecting something different. Then we ran the exact same play I'd called in the huddle, leading to another solid gain. The Citrus defense was spinning in circles over those new audibles, and Pisano had a grin on his face a mile wide.

I connected on another safe pass. Only, this time, Citrus had shifted its coverage off our receiver, turning a short gain into a long one. My elbow felt good enough. I'd found myself a groove. And most importantly, I was moving the chains, getting first down after first down, keeping Aiden on his bench.

A few plays later, we had reached the Citrus eighteen-yard line. I spotted a receiver turning open in the end zone, between a pair of defenders. The window wasn't big, so I knew I had to put some gas on the throw. I reared back and let the football fly, harder than I had in nearly a month. I felt that sharp twinge—but seeing the tight spiral speeding through the air made the pain worth it. Then I heard the *thhht* of the ball sticking in my receiver's hands.

"Touchdown!" I screamed, raising my arms up over my head.

I was starving for more. Two offensive series later, I had a good chance at tasting it again. I'd just sent the Citrus D into scramble mode with another audible. My protection was great, so I stood tall in the pocket waiting for a Beauchamp receiver to come free.

Suddenly, I spotted one of my receivers almost forty yards downfield, all alone. His defender must have fallen. My heart jumped—but a second later, I wished my teammate was ten yards closer. I reared back and prepared for the shock to my elbow, putting all of my weight behind the throw. Airing that ball out was like sticking a finger into an electric socket—*zap*.

I grimaced as the ball hung in the sky. My pass might have been five yards short. But my receiver made the adjustment, slowing down and coming back for it.

Then I dropped to my knees when the shock wouldn't subside.

The ball landed in my receiver's arms, and he streaked past the Citrus goal line, untouched. Even the intense satisfaction of a 14–0 lead couldn't match the pain I was feeling.

When I got to the sideline, I avoided everyone, including our trainer. I didn't want anybody bumping my elbow by accident. Taking a spot at the end of our bench, I slowly bent it at the joint, testing it out.

Out on the field, Aiden got lucky. Our defense had him under intense pressure in the pocket. One of our D-linemen even had an arm around his waist but couldn't bring him to the ground. Aiden stepped forward and threw the ball up for grabs. Downfield, two of our defenders got their feet tangled together as they leaped for it. They knocked each other over as the Citrus receiver made the catch and walked in for the score.

We had some luck run our way too. With less than a minute to go in the second quarter, I pitched the ball to our tailback, who swept wide to the right. The entire Citrus defense shifted outside to meet him, including whoever was supposed to stay at home in the middle of the field. That's when our runner saw a huge open seam and cut the play back inside.

There was nothing in front of him but eighty yards of green grass.

Those last twenty-five yards or so, as he turned on the after-burners just for fun, I glanced down at the *88* on my cleats.

No way he'll ever be as fast as you, fam, I thought.

At halftime, we had a 21–7 lead.

"Somebody go ask Aiden Conroy which locker room he'd rather be in right now," Pisano hollered.

Right away, I put my left elbow in a bucket of ice water, resting my helmet beneath my armpit. I tried to relax as best as I could, enjoying the score.

That's when Pisano said to me, "Nothing's really going their way on defense. Expect them to start blitzing and sending everybody after you. If I was coaching Citrus, it would absolutely be my plan."

"I know it's coming," I said, submerging my elbow a little deeper.

"Don't take any chances with the ball," Pisano continued. "We've got a nice margin. Just stay steady."

"I hear you," I said.

Pisano was right. The Citrus defense began blitzing me on nearly every play of the second half. Every time I dropped back to pass, I was under siege.

Citrus brought extra pass rushers off the right and left edges or sent linebackers through the gaps on our O-line. I played smart football, throwing a couple of passes out of bounds. I wasn't worried about stats or my QB ranking. It was all about winning, about beating Aiden Conroy and going 4-2, not 3-3.

In the third quarter, Citrus sacked me three times. But I bounced back after each one to show them those hits weren't anything, no matter how much they stung. Their D stopped responding to our audible keys. I guess their coaches had a new game plan—pummel the quarterback.

Sometimes I could see the blitzes coming and identified my hot receiver, who'd be left in man-to-man coverage. But my elbow still hurt from the forty-yard heave I had uncorked on my last TD throw, and now my passes were suffering from it.

Early in the fourth quarter, Aiden got another lucky break when one of our defenders missed a sure tackle on a short pass. The Citrus receiver went all the way for the score. Then, on the kickoff to us, our return man fumbled the football through the back of the end zone. That gave Citrus another gift—two more points on a safety.

In less than twelve seconds of game clock, our lead had been cut by nine points, down to 21–16. Aiden Conroy was only a touchdown away from me.

For a few seconds, every muscle in my body went super-tight, like they'd been stretched from goal line to goal line. So I picked up a ball and took some light practice throws. I didn't care about the pain. I just needed to feel the football coming out of my hand.

On the field, my passes were losing more and more steam, even when I put extra strain on my elbow. I concentrated on playing it safe, diffusing the Citrus blitzes with short swing passes and plenty of running plays. I was managing the offense and keeping us out of trouble. I hadn't put up any scores yet in the fourth quarter. But I was moving the chains, eating up the clock, and, most importantly, not committing turnovers.

That all became meaningless the next time Citrus had the ball.

I was standing on our sideline, chewing on my mouthpiece, when Aiden escaped the pocket. Some of the Bobcat defenders were out of position, and I dug my toes deep into the turf. Moving downfield, Aiden completely juked a linebacker. His fake was so smooth that even I leaned the wrong way for a split-second as Aiden cut past the defender.

Next, Aiden lowered his head, splitting a pair of tacklers and staying on his feet.

With a fifteen-yard gap between Aiden and the end zone, no one in black-and-gold stood ready to stop him. I closed my eyes, hoping he'd trip over one of the white lines. Or the ground would somehow open to swallow him up. But the reaction of our crowd let me know none of those things had happened.

I opened my eyes to see Aiden spike the ball and watched it bounce high into the air.

After that touchdown, Citrus lined up for a two-point conversion. I knew Aiden wasn't giving the ball up to anybody else, not after scoring on a run like that.

Sick to my stomach, I ran down the sideline toward our defense, screaming, "Quarterback keeper!"

Aiden barked, "Hut, hut," and sure enough, he kept the ball, pumping his legs and lowering his head again.

This time, Aiden met Cortez, who'd lowered himself even closer to the ground and stopped Aiden cold at the goal line. But that stop came one play too late.

I kissed two fingers on my left hand and touched them to the #88 on my cleats. Then I buckled my chin strap and went back onto the field. We were trailing 22–21—the game depended on whatever happened next.

"This is it. This is everything for me. I'm going to leave it all out here, every bit of what I got," I told the guys in my huddle. "Who's going to give me less than that?"

"Nobody," answered one of my linemen. The rest of them responded in kind.

I called the play and led us to the line of scrimmage, nearly eighty yards from a winning score. I scrambled to my left to avoid the blitz, delivering a short strike to my tight end. My elbow was on fire with the wrong kind of flames. But the throw gave us a nine-yard gain. Next, I handed the ball to our fullback, who got three yards up the middle for a first down, with the clock stopping for the two-minute warning.

"We need to get the ball inside their fifteen-yard line. Our field goal kicker is money from that close,"

Pisano said to me on the sideline. "Just move us along. If the receivers aren't open, throw the ball away."

Pisano gave me three consecutive plays to run, as we went to our no-huddle offense to save time.

I took the next snap and pump-faked a short pass. That bought me enough time in the pocket to find someone deeper downfield. But when I released the ball, it didn't move like the tight spiral I was expecting. Instead, the ball wobbled through the air like a wounded duck, bouncing off a defender's fingertips right into my receiver's hands for the ugliest eighteen-yard completion I could imagine. Thankfully, this wasn't about style points.

That messy pass play put us just past midfield into Citrus territory. Their blitz came at me full-force again. Pisano had called a delay draw, trying to sucker in the D-line. The defenders rushed forward, certain it was another pass play and ready to bury me. As they committed to that, I handed the ball off to our halfback. He sailed through a gaping hole, untouched, all the way down to the Citrus twenty-six-yard line.

There was 1:16 left on the clock.

My elbow felt almost numb as I ran Pisano's third play: another draw, this time with a different look, to our fullback. He powered the ball down to the twelve.

Right then, I was so confident, I felt like a tight-rope walker in a hurricane who wouldn't even admit the wind was blowing.

Fifty-two seconds left.

Citrus wasn't stopping for a timeout, and neither were we.

Pisano sent in a straight-ahead running play, trying to get us a little closer before our field goal attempt. As we approached the line of scrimmage, I could see our kicker warming up on the sideline out of the corner of my eye. Then I glanced at Aiden, who was staring right at me. The clock was down to thirty-nine ticks.

The Citrus defense looked heavy up the middle. On the outside, I had a receiver one-on-one with a defender he'd beaten all day. Deep down, I didn't trust our kicker. In my mind, he wasn't even a *real* football player. He'd come over from the soccer team.

I had too much riding on this game to leave it all on his leg.

I wanted at least one shot at a touchdown. So I called an audible.

"Tango, flyer, forty-four! Tango, flyer, forty-four!"

At the snap, I felt for the laces. Then I turned my eyes left and zeroed in on my receiver. It was either hit him clean on his break or throw the ball into the stands.

The defender got himself turned a half-step the wrong way. I reared back to put as much mustard on the ball as I could. But the instant my receiver was about to make his cut, he slipped.

I was already in mid-motion. My elbow was so tensed up, I couldn't hold back the throw.

The football floated toward the corner of the end zone while the Citrus defender regained his balance. My pass hit him high on the left shoulder pad. He juggled the ball, with my heart in his fingertips, before gaining control for an interception. Now I was the biggest loser by far.

When the final whistle blew, Aiden came over to shake my hand. I thought about hiding, but there was nowhere to go.

"Good game," Aiden said, putting his hand in mine.

I muttered the same words back, sweating enough to camouflage my tears, and prepared to face Coach Pisano and my teammates.

CHAPTER 28

I didn't take any more Tylenol. I wouldn't use ice or a heating pad. I dealt with the pain, alone in my room, because I felt like I deserved it. And I wouldn't even consider sending out a tweet.

Twenty minutes after I got home, Carter called my phone. The Gators didn't have a game that week, and he'd missed mine because he was studying.

"Mom made you call?" I asked.

"Not really. She told me what happened. I figured you'd need to talk."

"I know what you're going to say: 'Quarterback's ego. Think you're more important than the team.'"

"No, I just wanted to see how you were feeling. Let you know it's not the end of the world, just a football game."

"But I *gave* this one away. It was a big one," I said, glancing over at Carter's bed in the far corner, as if he were there.

"They're *all* big ones. So you messed up. Don't repeat

the same mistakes. That's why they call it *learning*."

"Sounds good, but it doesn't change things," I said, as new waves of pain and self-pity slammed my insides.

"Nothing changes things," Carter said.

"Then why am I even talking to you about it?"

"Because I might have answers to questions you didn't even know were coming. And if I don't have the answers, at least maybe I've seen the questions before."

"Anything else?" I asked, hoping to end the conversation.

"Just know that I'm here."

"I'll take it. But I wish there was more," I said, and then got off the phone.

The worst night of my life was when Dad left home. But this was right up there. I couldn't sleep. Pain and pressure came at me nonstop from every angle. What would Coach G. think about the way I blew the game—and my selfishness? And what if my elbow didn't come around?

* * *

Early the next morning, I got a call on my phone.

He wanted to meet me at a park close to my house. I was completely exhausted. But after everything he'd done to help me out, I felt like I couldn't turn him down.

I sat alone on a bench beneath a huge oak tree. There wasn't another soul in sight when he appeared.

"Saw some of your game last night."

"You did?" I asked.

"Enough to know that elbow isn't healing fast enough on its own."

"It's terrible. My passes have nothing on them," I said.

"That's why I think you need *these*," he said, pulling a vial of pills from his pocket.

"What are they?" I asked, trying to peer through the darkened plastic. "A new supplement?"

"Sort of. Just not approved yet. But they're completely undetectable to any test," he said. "I use them myself sometimes."

"So they're not legal?"

"Not for athletes, not without a prescription."

"You mean they're *steroids*?"

"Travis, steroids are *everywhere* in society. They're in the feed we give chickens and cows to make them healthier. These are for humans. In pill form, no needles. The mildest you can take. Just a few steps above aspirin or Tylenol. But instead of masking pain, they heal the problem at the source and promote growth," he said, pointing at my left arm.

I started to tremble on the inside. All I'd ever heard since the first grade was, *Just say no!*

"I can't. They're drugs," I told him, feeling some distance between us for the first time. "Anyway, it'd be cheating."

"I didn't mean to insult you," he said, putting the vial away. "I was only trying to help. It's what *plenty* of scholarship athletes do to compete when they're injured. I just wanted you to have the same options they do."

I made my excuses and then got out of there. I even turned down a ride.

By the time I walked home, the pain in my elbow was nearly unbearable. I waited for it to die down. It didn't. I was starving, but I couldn't even twirl leftover spaghetti around the fork.

This time, *I* called *him.*

I'd talked myself into believing I really wouldn't be cheating. That for me, taking steroids would be about getting healthy, not about becoming a better player. I already had the talent. That's why I had the scholarship in the first place.

A few hours later, we were back at that same bench. But now, he produced *two* vials of pills.

"It's a seven-week cycle," he explained. "The first four weeks, you take the ones in the container with the blue stripe. The next three weeks, take the ones from the red. They're stronger."

Before squeezing them tight inside my right hand, I almost laughed over the vials' child-proof caps.

When I got back home, I found a note on the kitchen table:

Hope you're feeling better. Took Galaxy to the dog-run for some exercise. See you in a couple of hours—Love, Mom

I locked my bedroom door behind me. Then I put both vials on top of my dresser and stared at them as my elbow throbbed.

It's almost the same as taking Tylenol, I told myself.

Dad rang my phone, but I wouldn't pick up. I didn't want to mix one set of problems with the other. I had too much sitting in front of me right now.

I must have walked twenty laps around the room, with my mind racing in a thousand different directions. Once I even stopped in front of my dresser and pushed down on the cap of the blue vial. I felt it give and knew it would twist open with one turn of my wrist. But just as quick, I took my hand back off.

Alex's face popped into my mind. What would he think of me taking a shortcut after how hard he worked to get his knee ready?

The trophies on the top shelf of my bookcase could have made up a team of golden football players. They looked down on me, like they were already passing judgment—only none of them had a dent or scratch on his body to worry about.

Something *he* said kept echoing in my ears: *It's what plenty of scholarship athletes do to compete when they're injured.* That definitely had me leaning toward trying the pills. I figured there was so much about big-time football I just didn't understand yet—maybe this stuff was totally common.

I turned around and noticed Carter's empty bed.

That's when it came to me. I could ask my brother for an honest answer about what college players did. Like Carter had told me, *If I don't have the answers, at least maybe I've seen the questions before.*

I put one of the vials in my pocket and hid the other inside a pair of sweat socks in my underwear drawer. Then I jumped on a city bus and headed down to the Gainesville campus.

I didn't call Carter until I was there.

"I've got a team meeting in about forty minutes. But come on up," he said.

Walking through the athletes' dorm with steroids felt strange. And every time the pills rattled inside my pocket, I looked around, paranoid that someone would hear them.

Carter met me at his door and asked, "How's your elbow? Looks like you can barely move it."

"I need to talk," I said. "I want to show you something, get your advice."

"On what?" he asked, closing the door.

I pulled the blue vial of pills from my pocket.

"Do you know anything about this kind of stuff?" I asked, with my voice dropping a couple of notches.

"Who gave you this crap?" Carter asked, snatching the vial away.

He looked so angry, I was afraid to tell him.

"I, I can't say."

"You don't have to. I've got my own ideas," he said, heading for the door.

A second later, he was bounding into the hallway and then starting down the stairs.

I chased after him, calling, "Come back, Carter! Please!"

But there was no stopping him.

Carter entered the football complex, with me on his heels. He marched past the pair of crystal footballs on display, through the sliding glass doors, and into the Gators' weight room. Coach Harkey was standing by a weight machine, studying some chart. That's where Carter grabbed him, running Harkey back against a wall.

"You! You did it!" Carter screamed, trying to shove that vial down Harkey's throat. "You gave these to Travis!"

Harkey managed to get his arms up, protecting himself.

"Are you crazy, Gardner?" Harkey hollered. "What are you saying?"

"It wasn't him!" I yelled, trying to pull Carter away with my good arm. "It wasn't Coach Harkey!"

Carter either didn't believe me or was too far gone to hear. Some Gators who'd been training tried to get between them. But Carter's grip on Harkey was solid.

"I'd never give a player steroids. Let alone a high school kid," said Harkey. "What kind of animal do you think I am?"

"Don't pretend with me!" Carter raged. "First you killed Alex, now you're pushing them at my brother!"

"It wasn't him!" I cried. "It was Walter Henry! He gave them to me!"

Carter slowly loosened his grip.

"Walter Henry," he said. The anger in Carter's eyes intensified until it turned to fire. "God, I should have seen it."

He pushed past everyone and darted out the door. Me and Harkey ran after him, but Carter got to his car in the parking lot before we could reach him. Then he sped off so fast, he left behind skid marks and the smell of burning rubber.

CARTER'S TAKE

I gripped the steering wheel tight, like it was Walter Henry's throat. I hated every second of being inside that car, being connected to anything that came from him. I was so geared up, I blew right through a stop sign and didn't notice until a van on a cross street came to a screeching halt.

"Stupid! Stupid! Stupid!" I pounded at the horn.

I wanted so much to go back in time, to change everything. But I couldn't. All I could do was speed that car through the streets, to Walter's dealership.

Walter was standing out front, talking to one of his salesmen. I aimed the car straight for him, jumping the curb. The salesman saw me bearing down on them first and took off. By the time Walter looked up, I was almost on top of him. He let out a scream—a real one, not a fake Tarzan-commercial scream. I slammed on the brakes, stopping just a few feet away, nearly pinning him against the glass of the showroom.

Walter was breathing hard by the time I stepped out

of the car, like he was about to have a heart attack.

"Are you insane, Carter?" he hollered. "You could have killed me!"

"Like how you killed Alex, giving him that trash?" I shouted.

I could see the look in his eyes. He couldn't deny it.

I grabbed Walter by the collar and rammed him against the hood of the car.

"Then you want to push that same garbage on Travis!" I shouted. "Explain that!"

"It wasn't the same, not even close," Walter said. "You've got to believe me. I never wanted anything but the best for Alex, for both of them."

"No, you only wanted the best for *you*," I told him, an instant before I punched him in the solar plexus.

Before I let myself do the wrong thing, before I split his skull open, I pulled him off the car's hood and shoved him inside the driver's door. Then I closed the door, picked up a garbage can, and smashed in the locks on both sides. After that, I took my keys and heaved them onto the dealership's roof. The last step was calling the cops—even though they were probably going to arrest me too.

CHAPTER 29

Dad wired us money, in case Mom had to post bail for Carter. But that wasn't necessary after Walter Henry refused to press any charges.

"I know exactly what he's thinking," Mom said, barely able to control her temper as we waited for the police to release Carter. "That if *he* doesn't press charges, *we* won't. But that's not going to happen. I don't care how much money he has or what kind of lawyer he hires. He belongs behind bars for pushing poison at my son."

Then she turned her anger toward me.

"And Travis Jerome Gardner," she said, hitting my middle name like a kick drum. "If I go into your dresser drawer, you're saying I'll find steroids that you brought into *my* home?"

"Yes, ma'am," I answered, with my eyes on that police station floor.

I was willing to take any punishment she gave me. My mind wasn't focused on me anymore, or the pain in my elbow. I wanted to talk to Carter about Alex. Right then, that was more important to me than anything else.

I guess Coach Harkey hoped for the same conversation with Carter. He was sitting in a row of straight-back wooden chairs maybe twenty feet from Mom and me, trying to give us some privacy.

He wasn't pressing charges against Carter either. In fact, when the campus police asked Harkey what had happened at the complex, he told them, "Nothing, just doing a blocking drill with one of my players."

Two officers accompanied Carter as he came out from behind a glass partition. I walked up to him before he reached Mom and stopped him from coming forward another step.

"Tell me about Alex. I have to know," I said.

Harkey appeared at my left shoulder, anxious to hear Carter's answer.

"I screwed up bad, real bad. I knew that Alex was taking steroids. But I kept my mouth shut about it," said Carter. "At first, I thought I was protecting Alex. Then I thought I was protecting his memory. But I didn't do either one of those things."

I put my hand on the center of his chest, like I could stop the guilt from pumping through his veins.

Part of me wanted to fall to the floor right there and cry like a baby. But another part of me sensed that Carter was carrying even more weight than I was. That I needed to be strong for him.

"What I really did was keep the door open for the same thing to happen to somebody else. And that somebody was almost you," Carter said. "If I'd have told the truth from the beginning, you never would have even thought about swallowing those pills. What if you hadn't come to me? What if you'd started doing it in the dark, like Alex? Made that decision on your own?"

"I never would have done that. I came to you because you're my fam. I knew I could trust you. Maybe it hasn't always been that way between us. But since Alex died, I felt like you've been looking out for me. Maybe more than anybody else."

But those vials had been right in my hands. I knew I'd felt the same kind of pressure to perform as Alex. It linked the two of us together—double-infinity.

That's when Harkey leaned in closer and said, "Relationships aren't easy. Lord, I only wish I'd had a better one with Alex Moore. Maybe he'd be here today if I did. But don't let anything break the bond that you two have—that bond between brothers. Not football, not anything."

Nobody had to tell me Harkey was right. I knew it in my heart.

CHAPTER 30

Detectives from the Alachua PD came to our house later that day. Mom let them inside, and Galaxy was on his best behavior. They took a statement from me about how Walter Henry gave me those steroids. Then they went into my room and confiscated the red-striped vial.

"We'll send the contents to the lab for analysis and examine the container for fingerprints," one of the detectives said.

"Will you be able to find Walter guilty over what he did to Alex Moore?" I asked. "That's all I really care about."

"Right now, that's just an accusation by your brother," the detective answered. "Unless there are others with information, or Mr. Henry decides that he can't live with his conscience and confesses, it's probably going to be difficult to prove."

I guess Walter pushed steroids at us so we'd play better. Then one day he'd cash in on a big commission as our agent. I couldn't make up my mind how I felt about what he'd done to me. In the end, I was the one who asked to take those vials of pills home. But I hated Walter's guts for what he'd done to Alex and his mother. And I wished to God I could have been there when Carter beat his behind.

Back in my room, I started thinking about how Alex lost his father too early, and what it had meant to him. I didn't want to just walk away from mine. I was still mad that Dad planned to stay in California. But I wasn't going to build a brick wall over it anymore. So I called him.

"I'm sorry, Travis. I let you down," Dad said. "I put too much trust in that Walter Henry character. I gave my blessing. I couldn't see him for what he really was—a user."

"That's all right," I said. "We were all blind to it."

"It's not going to happen again. I'm going to find a way to be more involved," Dad said. "I'm not going to let these sharks circle you."

"We'll find a way, no matter where you're living," I told him. "I'm just glad you're around."

Mom made an appointment for me with an orthopedist on Monday afternoon. That meant I wouldn't be going to football practice. I spent most of the night icing my elbow in the living room. It felt good to drop the act and stop pretending my left arm didn't hurt.

Before I went to bed, Carter showed up. Without his

car, he'd taken the city bus over. After spending all that time down at the police station, he'd gone back to the complex to face whatever fallout was coming.

"Just got out of a meeting with Coach G.," Carter told us. "He's suspending me for two games."

"Why?" Mom asked. "There are no charges against you."

"Somebody passing by the dealership took a video of me bashing my car doors with Walter Henry inside," Carter answered, looking depressed. "It's on YouTube as 'Grouchy Gator.'"

"Honey, I'm so sorry," Mom said. "Could you use a hug?"

Carter nodded his head.

When Mom hugged him, I did too.

My brother decided to sleep over that night. With my right arm, I dragged his bed out of the far corner of the room, moving it to where it belonged. We talked a lot about Alex and his life before we fell asleep. I could hear in Carter's voice how numb he must have been feeling. I wouldn't put the pain in my elbow within a hundred yards of how he probably felt.

I wondered if any of what had happened would hurt my scholarship. Thinking about it was tearing me apart inside. But I decided that right then, I had to walk away from worrying about myself. And even the next morning, I didn't mention my scholarship once to Carter.

The news about me and Walter and the steroids hadn't broken in the press. Outside of Carter and Mom, I kept it to myself. I didn't need anything else to explain to people, any other potential problems. For starters, on Monday, I had to face everyone at school over that interception.

Lots of kids were cold to me. I walked through the hallway with my eyes straight ahead, but I ran into Cortez in the bathroom.

"You're a quarterback. You're all about yourself. I shouldn't have expected anything more," he said, crumpling up a paper towel. "I wouldn't care, except it cost *us* the game."

That stung like anything to hear, and I couldn't argue against it.

"I get it," I said, trying not to show any emotion.

"Do you really? Or will you forget it the second you see yourself in that mirror?" said Cortez, pointing over the sink.

After Cortez had gone, and I'd finished my business, I washed my hands without ever looking up.

Damon was waiting for me outside one of my classes. I wasn't sure where he was headed next, but he hung around even after the late bell rang.

"Hey, I just wanted to tell you to stay strong," said Damon. "You'll get through this."

"Thanks, that really means something to me."

Even when I didn't have a football in my hands, Damon was still watching my back. I felt grateful—and promised myself that one day I'd be there for him too.

During PE, I'd told Pisano I couldn't make it to practice, explaining everything I'd been keeping from him about the elbow.

"Doctor's note," he said in a short voice. "Bring me one tomorrow without fail."

Then he stalked away, still angry over that audible I'd called.

The orthopedist Mom brought me to had a dozen photos in his office of him standing beside NFL players. So I knew that he'd treated the best.

He bent my elbow back slowly. "I can tell by the tension in the surrounding tissue what kind of pain you're in," he said. Before he even took an MRI, he added, "At best, it's my opinion that you shouldn't consider throwing a football for at least three or four months to let this heal."

That marked the end of my freshman season. And I had to admit, I was relieved to put that weight down.

-EPILOGUE-

Once I stopped throwing a football, the pain in my elbow really eased up. It was hard to feel almost healthy but still not be playing quarterback. I stood on the sideline for our home games wearing a sling on my left arm, signaling to the crowd that a doctor had grounded me. We got blown out in the first two games I sat out, with my backup playing horribly. Even though I wasn't on the field, some kids at school and guys on the team looked at me like I was to blame for the losses. That really spun my head around. So I talked about it with Ms. Orsini.

"When you're in the public eye, and you certainly are around here, people feel they know you," she said to me in her office. "They decide you owe them something for the attention they give you. But is it them you really owe something to, Travis?"

"No. I owe more to myself."

After our conversation ended, I started to wonder how much I owed Coach Goddard. He had practically made me who I was. Without Coach G. in my life, I'd have been somebody totally different.

But there was a time I felt like I owed Walter too—owed him something big. And I was completely wrong about that.

I was just getting a handle on all that when my entire world got kicked upside down again.

After Carter called the police on Walter, detectives investigating Walter's connection to Alex started looking at the dealership's sales records, including how many relatives of Gainesville Gators bought cars from the dealership. That all came out in the open when Karen Wolfendale wrote a story about those *special deals* for the *Sentinel*. Her story mentioned that the police were investigating Walter for supplying PEDs and his possible connection to Alex's death. Near the bottom, there was a whole paragraph about me and those two vials of pills. At the end, she put two and two together, explaining why Carter went off at the dealership.

I was worried about how Coach G. would react. Maybe the publicity backlash would make him walk away from me.

The article made Mom fume: "That reporter must have seen the police record. That's an invasion of our privacy. Travis is a minor. She shouldn't be allowed to print things like that. It could seriously hurt his future."

I was steamed over it too. Only Carter didn't have a problem with Wolfendale's story.

"I've had enough of sitting on the truth, trying to hide it," he said. "I'm not going to hold a grudge against somebody for getting the facts right."

"Think there could be trouble over the car I bought you?" Mom asked Carter.

"That's probably coming," he answered. "But I won't complain when it does. Not after the price Alex paid. You know what his mother said to me, after I told her everything? 'I'll let God judge my son's mistakes. That's what keeps my heart full of love, not anger.'"

The very next day, the NCAA announced a second investigation into Gator football players receiving illegal benefits. I thought the news couldn't get any worse. But it did, a few days later, when Mom showed me the headline on the front page of the paper:

GODDARD RESIGNS AS GATORS COACH.

I was shattered.

"I'm so sorry, Travis. Maybe Gainesville's athletic department will stand by the scholarship offer," she said, before I broke down crying in her arms.

An hour later, when I finally pulled myself together, I sent in a tweet, thanking Coach G. for the two national championships. But I got a message back from the media department at Gainesville saying the account had been shut down.

It was official. I was no longer @TravisG_Gator.

Carter called our house that afternoon and said,

"Coach G. is gone. He didn't even speak to the players. He just walked out. We heard he's talking to the Carolina Panthers about an NFL job as quarterback coach."

"What about Travis?" Mom asked him on speaker.

"Harkey said that without Goddard here, there is no scholarship."

"That's what I thought," I said.

"Coach Harkey had a message for you, though."

"Yeah, what?"

"He said for you to close your eyes and feel those raised letters on the weight room sign."

"Blood, sweat, and tears," I said, with the fingers on my left hand moving on their own.

"He didn't want you to forget that's what it takes," Carter said.

I couldn't believe Coach G. was out of my life.

* * *

Later that night, Dad called.

"There are ups and downs to everything worth having in life," he said. "You have to take the setbacks in stride, keep focused."

Calmness and execution jumped into my mind. But I wasn't going to talk over Dad with any words from some coach's mouth.

"I hear you, Dad," I said, actually meaning it for a change.

*   *   *

I didn't want to walk through the front door of Beauchamp High School without that scholarship. It defined who I'd become. Part of me felt like an absolute nobody. All those haters, everyone who'd ever been jealous of what I had, would line up to dump on me. And after the way I'd acted sometimes, I couldn't blame them for wanting to pump themselves up at my expense.

"You're exactly who you were before the scholarship," Mom told me as I left for school that first morning. "A great kid with a wonderful personality who loves football. And you're my son."

My entire body was on pins and needles as I swiped my ID card and entered Beauchamp. Ms. Orsini stood waiting for me outside my first-period class.

"You and I are going to meet twice a week during your lunch period," she said, handing me a schedule. "I want to know what's going on in your life on a regular basis—the good stuff, the bad stuff, the pressure, *everything*. Nothing held back. Deal?"

"Sure. And maybe we can start talking about what it's like to apply to colleges. The scholarship at Gainesville isn't going to happen," I answered, hearing myself say it out loud inside those walls.

"Not a problem," she said. "It's something we can work on together."

I thanked her. Then, as she was walking away, I

called back to her and said, "Ms. Orsini. I really mean thanks."

She just smiled and said, "I know."

If Mrs. Harper was anything, she was consistent.

"Good morning, Mr. Gardner. I'm glad to see you here and healthy," she told me as I entered her classroom. "I hope you have your math homework completed today."

I nodded to the part about the homework, happy to have escaped any kind of lecture from her on *absolute value*.

Later on, I sat with Lyn in the cafeteria. She didn't mention football until I did.

"Now that I'm not playing for a while, I'll need something else to do around school," I said.

"There's lots of stuff you could join," said Lyn. "Pingpong, drama, book club." Then she flashed a wide smile. "Maybe you could even become one of Mrs. Harper's mathletes."

I smiled at that myself before I took another bite of my sandwich.

When Pisano started talking *to* me again, instead of *at* me, he said, "Seems Goddard's resignation is the end of a dream for both of us."

I felt like popping off at Pisano, asking him what it was *he'd* lost. But I didn't. He was still the Bobcats' coach. And if my elbow let me, I might even be back at QB next season. If that's what *I* wanted.

Walter Henry pleaded not guilty to supplying me, a minor, with a controlled substance. He made bail, easy. After months of legal delays by his high-priced lawyer, the judge on the case still hasn't set a trial date. The DA hasn't charged him yet with anything connected to Alex's death. Meanwhile, that loser made a brand-new car commercial, one where he's the judge and jury. I've never seen it from start to finish because I change the channel every time it comes on.

The NCAA investigation hasn't concluded either. The newspapers said it could take another year before the process ends and people get their penalties. Carter cooperated fully with the investigation. He wouldn't tell me exactly what he'd said to them, just that he admitted making mistakes.

My elbow's coming along pretty good, feeling almost one hundred percent. I haven't thrown a pass in more than ten weeks. But every day, I spread my left hand across a football and grip the laces, to keep my strength up. Gainesville's athletic director barred me from the football complex, so I've been working out part-time with Damon to keep in shape.

One day in December, we took Galaxy on a jog through the park where we used to play football, running right by a game between a bunch of younger kids.

Their football got loose and bounced our way.

Galaxy pounced on it, stopping it from rolling with his nose, but he moved aside as I picked it up off the ground.

I smiled at Damon, then turned to the kid waiting for me to throw it back.

"Don't just stand there. Go deep."

AFTERWORD

Top Prospect was inspired by several real-life cases in which football players received high-profile scholarship offers from major college programs before entering high school. Among those players were quarterbacks Chris Leak (Wake Forest) and David Sills (University of Southern California) and defensive back Evan Berry (Tennessee).

In 1998, Coach Jim Caldwell offered North Carolina native Chris Leak a non-binding scholarship to Wake Forest University. Leak was an eighth-grader at the time. He went on to lead his high school team to three consecutive state championships before choosing to attend the University of Florida instead. In 2006, Leak led the Florida Gators to a National Championship. One year later, he played his first professional season with the Chicago Bears of the NFL. Leak then played for several teams in the Canadian Football League before ending his career in the Arena Football League. Leak later took a position on the sidelines, working as a wide receivers coach for his alma mater, UF.

Coach Lane Kiffin made scholarship offers to both Evan Berry and David Sills. In 2009, while coaching the University of Tennessee Volunteers, Kiffin offered a scholarship to fourteen-year-old Evan Berry, the younger brother of All-American Eric Berry (then a member of the Tennessee program). The next year, however, Kiffin moved on to coach the University of Southern California Trojans. In 2010, Kiffin once again went to the publicity playbook, offering a scholarship to thirteen-year-old quarterback David Sills. At the time, Kiffin, who saw Sills' YouTube workout video, had not met the young man in person.

"The scholarship offer has always been a dream of mine. I didn't want to give up a chance like that," David Sills told *Comcast Sports Network* at the time of the offer. "Other people don't like the commitment at a young age. But I think it's for the best right now . . . It does put a target on my back while I'm playing. But I'm just going to go out there and do what I can do."

The University of Southern California replaced Lane Kiffin in 2013, which invalidated any offer to Sills. Kiffin later became an assistant coach at the University of Alabama. In 2015, *Sports Illustrated* named Evan Berry an All-American based on his performance as a defensive back and fleet-footed kick returner. David Sills chose to join the University of West Virginia Mountaineers football program.

In 2014, the *New York Times* reported that fourteen-year-old soccer star Haley Berg was already weighing offers to attend several universities, making Berg one of the first female athletes to have her early offer publicized.

"When I started in the seventh grade, I didn't think they would talk to me that early," Berg told the *Times*. "Even the coaches told me, 'Wow, we're recruiting an eighth-grader.'"

Early scholarships may be more prevalent among female athletes than male athletes. In 2014, the National Collegiate Scouting Association, which helps athletes navigate the recruiting process, published numbers on offers made prior to an athlete's junior year in high school. For female lacrosse athletes, 36 percent of scholarships were early offers (compared to 31 percent for males). In soccer, it's 24 percent (8 percent for males), volleyball, 23 percent (18 percent for males), basketball, 18 percent (5 percent for males), and field hockey, 15 percent.

The NCSA reports that 4% of male football scholarships are early offers. Football is undoubtedly the lowest on the scale because it is difficult to forecast future success in the sport—one in which physical growth will influence an athlete's performance. Of course, in *Top Prospect*, the emotional growth of our protagonist is just as big a factor.

SPECIAL THANKS

April Volponi
Sabrina Volponi
Rosemary Stimola
Alix Reid
Greg Hunter

ABOUT THE AUTHOR

Paul Volponi is a writer, journalist, and teacher living in New York City. From 1992 to 1998, he taught incarcerated teens on Rikers Island to read and write. That experience helped to form the basis of his award-winning novels *Black and White* and *Rikers High*. Paul is the author of twelve young adult novels, including *The Final Four* and *Game Seven*.

He holds an MA in American literature from the City College of New York and a BA in English from Baruch College.

Visit him at www.paulvolponibooks.com.